SUPER SWEET 13

candy apple books... just for you.

SUPER SWEET 13

by Helen Perelman

SCHOLASTIC INC.

New York   Toronto   London   Auckland
Sydney   Mexico City   New Delhi   Hong Kong

ISBN 978-0-545-16284-5

12 11 10 9 8 7 6 5 4 3 2 1   10 11 12 13 14 15/0

Printed in the U.S.A.   40
First printing, March 2010

For Mom and Dad

Special thanks to my "thirteen" advisors (past and future) — Jessica Perelman, Andrew Perelman, and Sam Spector. And to the sweet and gracious Shannon Penney for all her help planning and plotting this super party.

CHAPTER ONE

I knew from the moment I walked into the Riverhouse Café that it was the absolute perfect spot for my big thirteenth birthday party.

At Career Day last month, Kara Miller's mom had told us all about her fancy party-planning business and how she could get a feel of a place right away. I knew what she was talking about as soon as I walked into the back room of the Riverhouse.

"Look at this huge dance floor!" I cried when I saw the open area. "This is exactly what I wanted! Isn't it great?" I spun around and smiled at my two best friends, Lara Abrams and Becca Sanchez. They were both nodding in complete agreement. I twirled around in the center of the dance floor.

Even though there was no music playing, I could imagine the beat pulsing through speakers around the room.

"Look at all the lights," Becca said. "It's like being onstage!" She walked, staring up at the ceiling. Her mouth hung open a little bit, and I couldn't help giggling.

"Check out the couches," Lara squealed as she plopped down onto a plush red love seat. "They're totally A-list!"

"This is so perfect!" I declared.

Lara joined me on the dance floor. "You're going to have the best thirteenth birthday party ever," she sang out.

I took her hand and spun her around as Becca danced over to us.

Party planners like Mrs. Miller knew all the cool places to host an event, and they knew about all the details that would make it a huge success. Kara had a big blowout when she turned thirteen — she's two years older than me, but I heard all about it from my friend Mariah Ryder's older sister. She told me about the amazing band (they had played at the Kids' Choice Awards) and the two different dresses that Kara wore for the party.

If only I had someone like that to help me plan my thirteenth birthday party.

I just had my parents. And they were definitely *not* party planners.

Not even close.

My mom's idea of a fancy party was putting on real shoes instead of flip-flops. And my dad thought that pizza was the ideal party food.

So for my thirteenth birthday, I had to take matters into my own hands.

After all, thirteen was different.

Thirteen was the start of a whole new world.

And in order to usher in that new world order, I wanted a party. A big party with music and dancing, fancy food, and dressed-up guests. No flip-flops. No jeans. No pizza. Since I didn't have a party planner, I had to do all the research myself. I spent most of my winter break poring over magazines and websites, and putting the information into my purple party-planning notebook.

From the center of the dance floor, I could see my mom standing in the doorway, talking to the manager of the Riverhouse. I hoped that she'd agree that this was the perfect place.

"So what do you think, Carly?" my mom asked, walking over.

"I love it!" I told her. "Don't you?" I held my breath.

My mom nodded. "This does seem to have everything you were looking for," she said, peering around. "There's a large dance floor, twinkling lights, and they don't serve pizza."

She was right — those were my top requests for the party space. I wanted to make sure that this party was more sophisticated than the ones I'd had in the past. For my other birthdays, my friends and I would gather in our basement and have pizza and ice-cream cake. This year, I was ready for a change.

I bounded over to my mom and gave her a hug.

At a place like this, my thirteenth birthday party was guaranteed to be perfect.

The next morning at school, I walked into English class with Lara and Becca. We had only two classes together, English and social studies. Luckily, we had lunchtime to catch up on the day's news, too.

"I heard your party is going to be at the Riverhouse," Mariah said as she slid in the desk behind me.

Good news travels fast — that's for sure.

"Yes," I said with a grin — trying to sound casual.

"My cousin had her graduation party there," Mariah said. "Did you know they have a bubble machine? So cool."

Hmm, a bubble machine? I took out my purple notebook and wrote that detail down. I'd have to ask Sylvia, the manager of the Riverhouse, about that.

"Hi, Mrs. Chaiken," Alex Sawyer said as he sped into class just before the bell rang. He quickly took off his baseball cap and put it under his chair. Mrs. Chaiken didn't allow hats in class, and he knew the drill. Alex turned and flashed me his new brace-filled smile. Unlike other kids in seventh grade, Alex had been excited to get braces. He even got blue wires for the Yankees, his favorite baseball team.

I couldn't help smiling back as I gave a little wave. Alex was totally baseball-crazed. He'd been that way since nursery school. We met in the sandbox on our first day at Cleary Preschool. (He had been wearing a baseball hat, of course.) Alex was different from the other boys in my class — he was really my friend. I didn't get nervous around him, or worry about acting cool. Unfortunately, he wasn't on the traveling soccer team with Greg Weiss, Ryan Shaw, Max Leary, and Drew Wyatt (sigh). Maybe if he was, I would have been friends with those guys, too.

Drew Wyatt was new to Jefferson Middle School. He arrived in October, and I couldn't help crushing on him. He had dark hair that swept over his forehead, and green eyes. I got to see him three times a day — in English, social studies, and gym. Sometimes I would catch myself staring at him during lunch (how embarrassing!), and I'd even think about going over to talk to him. But then he joined the indoor soccer league and started sitting with Greg, Ryan, and Max (the most popular and cutest boys in our class!). At least if he'd been sitting with Alex, I *could* have casually gone over and said hello. No such luck.

I didn't tell Lara and Becca about my crush. Somehow, I was sure that admitting my crush on Drew would make things too real and weird. After all, I didn't want to jinx anything.

I'd already decided that my birthday party would be the best way to bring us together. I loved to dance, and I was pretty good. I've taken classes since I was three years old. So I imagined that under the sparkling lights at the Riverhouse, I'd confidently ask Drew to dance, and of course he'd say yes. Who wouldn't want to dance with the birthday girl? Twirling around the floor, we'd have one of those magic moments — the ones you always see in movies and on TV. He'd totally fall for me! (Hey, it *could* happen.)

As I sat in class, I thought about the list of names folded up in my notebook. Now that I had a place for the party, I had to come up with the guest list. If this was going to be the party of the year, I needed to have the right people there.

"Everyone, take out your journals, please," Mrs. Chaiken said. "We'll begin with ten minutes of writing."

"I'm going to write about the baseball draft," Alex called out.

Mrs. Chaiken gave him a stern look. "Please raise your hand."

I rolled my eyes. If Alex could get away with thinking only about baseball 24/7, he'd be a happy guy. As I stared at the blank page in my journal, I smiled. I was no better than Alex — I had a one-track mind, too. All I could think about was planning my birthday party! I had lots of reasons to make sure that this party was a success.

I glanced across the room at Drew. He was hunched over his journal, writing.

Reason number one.

CHAPTER TWO

"How many people are you going to invite?" Becca asked. She opened her locker and piled her books inside. After all the excitement of finding the right place for the party the day before, I wasn't surprised that she wanted to get down to the important details right away. That's Becca for you.

"I'm not sure," I said. "Since I want there to be lots of dancing at the party, I need to have about the same number of boys and girls."

"Hmm," Becca said with a dreamy look in her eyes. She tossed her long, straight black hair over one shoulder and sighed.

I knew she was already thinking of boys that

she'd want to dance with at the party. Becca was totally boy-crazy. She had more crushes than Lara and me combined!

"You should definitely invite Ryan and all his friends," Becca said. Her dark eyes sparkled when she mentioned his name. "Ryan's a fantastic dancer. Remember how he danced at Greg and Mindy's party?"

We all nodded. Greg and Mindy Weiss's B'nai Mitzvah was last month. The twins had a DJ, and practically the whole grade was invited. Mindy danced with every boy at the party (even Ryan). She was a total star that day, and so was her brother. Before their party, I never even knew that Greg could dance.

"You have a crush on Ryan?" Lara asked, bumping Becca with her elbow. "I think that brings your boy tally to over twenty!"

"Oh, who's counting?" Becca countered, grinning. "Why? Do you like Ryan, too?"

"Well, kinda." Lara giggled, and her face got bright red. Lara is really fair, and when she blushes her whole body turns tomato red — even her freckles! She glanced around the hallway, making sure no one was listening to her crush confession.

"We know," Becca said, grinning, "your real crush is Max."

Lara's red face deepened a shade. "Well, yeah. He's just so funny! He's always cracking jokes and making me laugh."

"I'm not really friends with Ryan," I said quietly, feeling a little shy about inviting the cutest boy in seventh grade to my party.

"Of course you're inviting him!" Becca said, full of confidence. "He always says hi to you."

"He says hi to everyone," I said, pointing out an obvious fact. "He's just a friendly guy."

"Exactly the kind of guy that you want to have at your dance party," Lara said, nudging me.

"This is the perfect opportunity to act on any crush that you have," Becca said. "You might even get to dance with him!"

I had to admire Becca's attitude. She was always so sure of herself. Maybe it came from all her theater experience. Last year she was Frenchie in *Grease*, our school show. It was a big deal that a sixth grader got one of the leads, but she's that good. If she wasn't one of my best friends, I'd be incredibly jealous of her.

I wished that I were as confident as Becca. I could never stand center stage and sing, and I definitely couldn't just walk up to Ryan and talk to him . . . not to mention dance with him!

Becca leaned in closer. "And I know you may not want to hear this," she whispered, "but maybe you should think about inviting Dylan, Jordyn, and Marty."

Lara gasped. "Becca!" she scolded. "Are you kidding? You can't be serious."

"I'm totally serious," Becca said, shrugging. "You should just consider it. We could handle them."

I shook my head. Dylan, Jordyn, and Marty might have boys' names, but those girls were one hundred percent *all girl*. In fact, they were the most popular trio in the seventh grade — and the biggest snobs. I scanned the hallway, making sure they weren't nearby. They were *not* on my invite list. Nowhere near it!

"Ryan and his friends would come to your party without those three phonies," Lara objected. "I say you should only invite the people you want."

I smiled at Lara. "Thanks. I really wasn't planning on having the Royal Trio at my party," I said, sticking my nose in the air. "I see enough of them at school, thank you very much."

I could see Becca's point. Those girls were usually hanging out with Ryan and his group — but this was *my* party.

Becca held up her hands in surrender. "All right, all right," she said, smiling. "It was only a suggestion."

"Come on," Lara said, closing her locker. "My mom is waiting for us. We only have an hour at the mall."

"Can we get smoothies first?" Becca pleaded as we headed down the hall. "I can't shop on an empty stomach."

Twenty minutes later, the three of us were sitting in the mall food court with smoothies in our hands. I pulled out my guest list and put it on the table.

Lara looked down at my list. "You have to invite Alex," she said. "He'd be heartbroken if you didn't!"

I threw a napkin at Lara. "Alex and I are just friends," I said firmly. "Besides, he's already on the list." I pointed out his name.

Just then, Lara squinted over my head. "Well, well, look who it is. The Royal Trio is at the Smoothie Shack right now."

Becca and I both turned to look behind us, following Lara's gaze. There they were — Dylan,

Jordyn, and Marty — all wearing the same black leggings and sweater dresses, cinched with wide belts.

Lara, Becca, and I never wore the same thing. Lara always looked as if she'd just stepped out of a catalog. She wore outfits that looked professionally styled, right down to her shoes. Actually, half of Lara's closet was stacked with shoes. She was a true fashionista.

Becca had a totally different style. Her favorite color was black, and she usually wore short skirts with leggings instead of pants. I could never pull off that look, but she always looked great.

Glancing down at my outfit, I realized that I wore pretty much the same thing all the time: my favorite jeans and some version of a long-sleeved T-shirt. Boring.

The Royal Trio was all about the same size. To me, they always looked like a group of backup singers in a band. If they weren't matching, they were all wearing a similar ensemble. They definitely texted one another before they left the house to coordinate outfits — that much was obvious.

As I watched them, Marty suddenly locked eyes with me. Her glare was as chilly as that first sip of a frozen smoothie.

I used to be friends with Marty — best friends.

But that was a long, long time ago. We had nothing in common anymore, except the same social studies and gym teachers. From my plastic food court seat, I could see her dark eyes narrow and her glossed lips purse before she turned around.

She leaned over to whisper in Dylan's ear . . . and pointed right at me.

I glanced away, picked up my Smoothie Shack cup, and took a long, chilly sip.

"Oh, good," Lara said a moment later. "They're leaving."

"They need to shop for more matching outfits," Becca muttered, snickering.

I watched the three girls descend on the escalator, away from the food court. Happy that they had left, I turned back to my friends and took my party-planning notebook from my bag. Back to business!

"Now that I have a place for the party, I've got to come up with a theme." I pulled my straw up, then pushed it down through the hole in the orange plastic top. "The party theme sets the tone," I said, reading a quote from one of the articles I'd pasted in my notebook.

"And then there are the centerpieces and party favors," Becca said, leaning over my shoulder. "Greg and Mindy had those stuffed animals and soccer balls in the center of the tables at their party, and they gave out cute sweatshirts, remember?"

"Just please, no Fairytopia!" Lara blurted out.

I laughed so hard that I nearly choked on my smoothie gulp. "Oh, I'm not going to do that again!" I said, after I recovered from gagging.

Becca looked confused. I always forgot that she wasn't in elementary school with Lara and me. I put my hand on her arm.

"So, in first grade I was a little obsessed with Barbie Fairytopia." I shook my head. "You know, we look so much alike," I added, smiling. "Don't you think?" With my brown wavy hair and dark eyes, I had no resemblance to Barbie or her character, Elina, in the Fairytopia series. But when I was six, I really thought that I could be her. "I wore this one Fairytopia shirt to school every day for months," I confessed to Becca. "My parents went along with it. I even made them call me Elina."

"Wow," Becca said, smiling. "I never would have pegged you for a Barbie girl."

"Oh, I was," I said. "But you'll be happy to know that I've moved on."

Becca wrinkled her nose. "I was really into the Bratz." She covered her face with her hands. "And

I still have a bunch of them in a box in my closet!" she confessed.

We all burst out laughing.

"Hey, look," Becca said, her voice taking on a more serious tone. "Ryan, Greg, and Max are here, too."

I looked where Becca was pointing, and saw the three boys eating pizza at a table across the food court.

"Should we go over and say hello?" Becca dared us.

Lara turned red, and I shook my head, hard. It was one thing to send a party invitation to those boys . . . but it was a whole other thing to walk over to their table at the mall!

"Becca!" Lara squealed. "You're serious?"

Becca cocked her head to the side. "Why not?"

I could think of a thousand reasons not to walk over there, but apparently Becca wasn't considering any of them. She got up and headed straight for the boys' table! But just when I thought she was going to make contact, she went over to the big orange trash can and dumped her Smoothie Shack cup in the garbage.

I couldn't help laughing.

"Nice move," I said as Becca plopped back down in her seat at our table.

"I would have gone over," Becca said coyly, "if you would have come with me!"

As we watched (subtly, of course), the boys got up and headed for the escalator. They disappeared into the mega music store on the first floor.

"What about music for a theme?" Lara asked, suddenly inspired.

"That's a fantastic idea!" Becca said.

Becca was really into music. Not only did she star in musicals at school, she also played the piano *and* the cello. I used to take piano lessons, but I could never play like her. Becca was a natural talent. She could sit down at the piano and play a song that she had just heard on the radio.

"You could make music notes and pictures of instruments as your centerpieces," Becca went on. "Oh, and you could burn a CD as a party favor!"

I thought about it for a minute. "Yeah, that's a good idea," I said. "But that sounds like you, not me."

Lara and Becca nodded in agreement.

"What about a shopping theme?" Lara offered. "You could have shopping bags filled with clothes and cool stuff on the tables."

"Now, that definitely sounds like *you!*" I said, laughing.

Lara shrugged. "Maybe I'll do that for my party, *if* I ever have a party." She pouted. "I hate being the youngest in our class. I won't turn thirteen until eighth grade!"

"How about movies?" Becca asked, turning back to party ideas. "You love movies!"

She was right about that — I did love movies, especially romantic comedies. The cheesier, the better! I had a whole DVD library under my bed. Last fall when I had the flu, I'd rated and labeled all of them. (I gave four hearts for a stellar romance and one heart for the ones that were just okay.)

I flipped to a clean page in my party notebook and wrote down the movie idea. It wasn't perfect, but it was a good start.

"But what would the centerpieces be? And the party favors?" Lara asked. She wrinkled her nose. "How about a vacation theme? You could have a centerpiece that showed skiing, and another one about the beach . . ."

"Hmmm, maybe," I said, jotting that idea down, too. Mrs. Chaiken always says that writing down ideas is an important part of brainstorming. I tapped my pen on the notebook. The list was short so far, and I wasn't seeing any real possibilities.

"What about animals?" Becca asked, perking up. "You love animals. Especially dogs. That could be really cute. You could blow up a photo of Barney!"

Barney was my German shepherd. He was the sweetest dog, and I loved him. We got him when I was nine years old.

"I thought about that," I said, resting my chin in my hand. "But I think it's too close to what Mindy and Greg did for their party. Remember they had pictures of Rufus, their dog? I want to do something special and different."

"What about tennis?" Lara said, her blue eyes wide-open. "That is *so* you!"

"The boys would all love it," Becca added.

"Hmmm," I said as I considered the idea. "But it's not really glamorous," I said, chewing my pen cap.

Lara nodded. "Finally willing to trade in your sneakers for some high heels, huh?" A wide grin spread over her face.

I laughed. "Well, I'm not sure about heels, but I'm definitely not wearing sneakers to this party."

Becca peered over my shoulder at my theme list. "This is kinda hard," she said. "But at least you're having a party. There's no way my parents are throwing me a big party." She took a long sip of her smoothie. "Plus, my birthday is during the summer, when we're away at the lake house."

I grinned at my two best friends. "This party is for all of us," I said. "It's to start our thirteenth year, *together*."

I raised my smoothie cup to make a toast.

"Here's to turning thirteen!" I said. "And to a totally amazing party!"

"With an amazing theme!" Becca added.

Lara looked at me and winked. "We'll think of one, don't worry." As always, she had a way of saying things so that I believed her.

"Maybe we should walk around and look for more inspiration," Lara said, standing up. "Shopping always inspires me." She reached down and slung her huge pocketbook over her shoulder. Lara always carried a bag that looked as if she were about to go on a weeklong sleepover. The crazy thing was, she could find anything in there in five seconds flat. Impressive!

"Good idea," I agreed. As I walked over to the garbage can to throw away my smoothie cup, it suddenly hit me. The answer to my problem was right in front of me! How could I not have thought of it before? Sure, I loved tennis, movies, and dogs, but there was one other thing I couldn't live without.

I spun around and grinned at my friends.

"She's definitely got an idea," Lara said. "Look, she's about to burst!"

"Spill it," Becca ordered.

Pointing straight ahead, I directed my friends to the perfect theme. It was fun, colorful, cool, and definitely very me: Candy World, the biggest and brightest candy store in the mall.

"Brilliant!" Becca cheered. "Everyone loves candy!"

"Especially you," Lara added. "Carly's Candy — it's the perfect theme!"

CHAPTER THREE

"Olivia!" I yelled. "Hurry up — you've been in there forever!" I pounded my fist on the bathroom door. "Come on!"

"Okay, okay," Olivia called through the closed door. "I'll be fast."

My little sister was many things, but fast was not one of them. Ever since Olivia turned ten, she'd become a total princess. She'd deleted all evidence of her passion for soccer. Now she was all about fashion.

It was much easier to deal with her when she was a jock.

The only time Olivia moved quickly was first thing in the morning ... so she could get in the shower before me. That was how important blow-drying her hair was to her. The girl would give up sleep in order to dry her curls straight.

We had the same thick wavy hair, but she always blew hers stick straight. And her hair was blond, like my mom's. I had my dad's dark hair and eyes. When you looked at the two of us, you couldn't even tell that we were sisters.

I stomped back to my room and slipped under the covers. I couldn't go back to sleep, and waiting for the bathroom door to open was torture. My school started twenty minutes earlier than Olivia's. I should have first bathroom privileges every morning, but the darling princess always snagged the time slot before I could open one eye.

Barney rushed into my room and jumped up on my bed. Even though he was a full-grown dog, he still acted like a puppy.

"Hello, Mr. Barney," I said, rubbing his neck. "Yup, she snuck in first again."

Barney barked and wagged his tail.

At least someone in my family understood my pain.

Finally, the bathroom door clicked open, and I headed back into the hallway. Olivia stood there with a soft pink towel wrapped around her body, and another wound tightly on her head.

"All yours," she said, grinning.

"You *know* that I'm supposed to shower first," I said, pushing past her.

"You snooze, you lose," Olivia shot back, smirking.

"She's right, Carly," my mom chimed in, reaching the top of the stairs. She looked at her watch. "You'd better hustle."

After I raced through my shower, I quickly got dressed and headed downstairs. I had some party business to discuss with my parents before school.

"Candy girl, you are my world," my dad sang when I walked into the kitchen. He grabbed my hand and twirled me around. I recognized the old Jackson Five song, even though my dad's singing wasn't all that great. He's always been really into old Motown songs. It's kind of embarrassing when he's driving me and my friends somewhere and he bursts into song.

Then again, his singing is not nearly as embarrassing as his dancing.

As I watched him dance around the kitchen, I realized that I probably should have thought about that before I started campaigning to have a dance party. I wasn't sure how I'd be able to keep my dad off the dance floor — or keep him from totally embarrassing me!

"Daaad," I said, rolling my eyes.

He brought his hands to his chest as if I'd wounded his heart. "Aw, you won't dance with me?" He did one of his signature spins that ended in a "ta-da!" pose.

My mom cracked up. "You can't stop him, Carly," she said, dancing over to him. My dad twirled her around. "You just have to join him!"

I tried not to groan as I slumped into a seat at the kitchen table and poured myself a bowl of cereal. I was definitely going to need to set up some rules for the party. Rule Number One: no parents on the dance floor!

Barney raced around my parents, barking. He seemed to understand the embarrassing implication of disco-dancing dads.

"I think that Carly's Candy is going to be a great theme, honey," my mom said, bopping around the kitchen with my dad. "It's really perfect for you."

"Thanks," I said, trying to ignore the goofy dance moves. "I've already started making a list of my favorite jelly bean flavors."

My mom smiled. "Jelly beans will make a

perfect favor. And I bet we can come up with some great ideas for the invitations, too."

"And don't forget the centerpieces," my dad piped up. "Those are so important to the theme." A sly grin spread across his face.

I knew my dad was making fun of me. But all these party details were important! "This isn't funny, Dad," I said, trying to sound grown-up and official. "I want everything to be perfect."

"Well, that's not going to happen," my dad said matter-of-factly. "Haven't you ever heard your mother talk about our wedding?"

My mom flung a dish towel at my dad, laughing. "Oh, please," she said. "That was so different."

I *had* heard about the huge rainstorm that happened on the night my parents got married. They planned to have the ceremony outside at the Botanical Gardens, but the storm forced them to move indoors.

"And the moral of that story," my mom said, coming up behind me, "is that even though the ceremony went differently than we planned, it was beautiful." She gave my dad a kiss.

Ugh.

Come on, people! I wanted to shout. *Enough of*

the public displays of affection here! We were definitely going to need to set some ground rules before the party.

"We have to order invitations this week," my mom said, turning back to me. "Have you thought about those yet? Some brightly colored lollipops would be cute."

"But I want something cool, not *cute*," I clarified.

My mom held up her hands, smiling. "Okay, then," she said. "I guess that you've given this some thought. I made an appointment with Mrs. Dawson from down the street for this afternoon."

I knew Mrs. Dawson. She had a huge garden at the edge of her property. Barney loved to sniff around there, and whenever I walked him, we had to cross the street so he wouldn't dig up her flowers.

"She sells invitations from her house," my mom explained. "It seems like she has quite a few designs that could work for a candy theme. How's the guest list shaping up?"

I was one step ahead of her. Lara, Becca, and I had worked hard all week to craft the perfect guest list. I reached into my backpack and pulled out my party-planning notebook.

"I've already made a guest list for the party," I said proudly. I handed my mom the list . . . and watched her eyes grow wide.

"There are a lot of names here," my dad said as he peered over my mom's shoulder. "Carly, we're not hosting a wedding." Suddenly, he wasn't joking around anymore.

I gulped down a spoonful of cereal and scowled into the milk. There weren't *that* many people on the list. What did my parents expect? This was supposed to be the party of the year.

The list appeared in front of my cereal bowl.

"Take another look," my mom said calmly. "You need to cut this list. We aren't inviting your entire grade."

I wanted to point out that the whole grade was most definitely *NOT* on the list. For starters, I had made sure not to include the Royal Trio: Jordyn, Dylan, and Marty. I guess the list *was* padded with a few extra people — people I didn't actually talk to on a daily basis. But this was a party!

By definition, a party meant lots of people . . . didn't it?

I picked up the list and scanned the names. "How many people are you thinking?" I asked, trying to sound cool and calm. "This is my thirteenth birthday, you know."

"I'm very aware of that," my mother said flatly. "Less than half of that list." She didn't raise her voice. She didn't even bat an eyelash. She was serious.

But that didn't mean I had to agree.

"I spent a lot of time on this," I said quietly, swirling the last Cheerio around in my bowl. I watched as it bobbed up and down in the milk. "It's not easy to make a list."

"I know," my mom said. "And it will be even more difficult to cut it, I'm sure. But the Riverhouse can't accommodate all those people." She wasn't budging.

I folded up the list and slid it back into my party-planning notebook, trying not to sigh out loud.

My dad winked at me. "You'll figure it out," he said. "No one likes a crowded dance floor, anyway."

But that didn't make me feel better. I had no idea how I was going to chop the list. Didn't my mom understand that people came in clusters? If I invited Mindy and Mariah, I'd have to invite Zoe and Alyssa. I couldn't invite Greg without inviting Ryan and Max. And I really wanted to invite Drew! Would he come if Greg, Ryan, and Max weren't there? Would he know I had a crush on him if I didn't invite his friends? The list was like a giant mathematical problem. I'd never liked math much.

I sulked through the rest of breakfast.

By the time I stopped at Lara's for our walk to school, I was about to explode. I waited on the sidewalk in front of her house, clutching the list of names. Lara jogged down her front steps, her large bag slung over one shoulder.

"My mom vetoed the list," I said before Lara even had a chance to say hello.

"What?" She stopped walking and stared at me, her mouth gaping open. Lara had a flare for the dramatic, but at moments like these I appreciated it. We had spent *hours* finding the right balance for the party guest list!

"I need to cut the list in *half*," I said.

"Whoa," Lara replied as we headed down the sidewalk, side by side.

I glanced over at her. "I'm not sure how I'm going to fix this," I said.

Lara put her arm around me. "Don't worry, we'll do it together."

I smiled at my best friend. I was glad that she was there for me . . . but I wasn't sure if anyone could really help. The party of my dreams was already turning into a nightmare!

*   *   *

In Mrs. Bloom's social studies class, I carefully surveyed my classmates before the bell rang. I drummed on my purple notebook with my fingers, thinking about who I could leave off the party list. Mariah was talking to Zoe and Alyssa. I considered taking them all off the list, but I'd gone to Mariah's sleepover last month. I couldn't *not* invite her. Cutting this list was like untangling wires on an explosive. One bad cut could blow my chances for having a great party! (Not to be dramatic or anything.)

Across the room, I watched Drew copy down the homework assignment from the board. He looked so cute, with his dark hair swinging down in front of his eyes. He definitely wouldn't come to the party without Ryan, Greg, and Max. I sank lower into my seat.

"Please take out your homework assignments," Mrs. Bloom said, snapping me back to attention. She rolled a piece of chalk in her hands as she walked around the room. The chunky silver rings on her fingers made clinking noises as she wove in and out of the rows of desks. "I'm very excited to read your cultural essays. Please pass them to the front of the room."

Dylan's hand shot up right in front of Mrs.

Bloom's face. "You're going to love my essay," she boasted loudly. "My father took me, Marty, and Jordyn to the ballet. We had box seats. You know, the *best* seats? And after the show, we met the ballerina. She was from France."

"Very nice," Mrs. Bloom replied.

Marty and Jordyn both nodded. I wondered if there were strings attached to their heads, so they would all move the exact same way.

I tried not to roll my eyes. At least I knew three names that were *staying* off the list. Our cultural essays were supposed to be about an aspect of culture in our neighborhood, not a personal statement about what we did over the weekend — or an excuse to brag. Ugh.

"My essay is about baseball," Alex yelled out. "Pitchers report for spring training in a few weeks!" He pumped his fist high in the air.

Mrs. Bloom shook her head. "Alex, please raise your hand before answering," she said, her lips slightly pursed together. She did that a lot when Alex called out answers.

I smiled at Alex. I knew he was just excited. The guy lived for the baseball season. He kept these crazy charts and followed all the games. He was a true fan.

"That's not culture," Dylan said, wrinkling her nose.

I looked over at Becca and Lara, trying to get their attention to make a face. But my friends were staring at Ryan and Greg with big, goofy smiles on their faces. I couldn't help but giggle. They were definitely crushed out!

Mrs. Bloom pursed her lips tighter. "Did anyone write about the renovation of the old cinema on Main Street?" she asked, trying to direct the class back to the assignment.

"I did, Mrs. Bloom," Drew said, handing her his assignment. "They're showing a Godzilla movie now. The special effects were kinda lame, but it was cool."

"Those old movies are fun to watch," Marty chimed in, smiling at Drew. I watched her bat her long lashes at him, and tried not to gag. As if she would ever set foot in a Godzilla movie — Marty was afraid of the Wicked Witch music in *The Wizard of Oz*! One time when she slept over years ago, we watched that movie and she freaked out. I had to fast-forward every time the music started.

But at that moment in social studies class, I realized something truly scary. Marty was wearing the same goofy grin as Becca and Lara.

Since when did Marty have a crush on Drew?

"Yeah, it was cool," Drew said, smiling. He turned back around in his seat to face the front of the room.

Jordyn and Dylan both giggled into their hands. I wanted to throw up. How could Marty and I have a crush on the same boy? We were like oil and water. Clearly, Drew couldn't like us both — we were way too different.

"We're beginning a new unit today," Mrs. Bloom announced to the class, cutting into my thoughts. "For the next five weeks, we're going to research a few different countries around the world. We'll break into groups, and each group will have to come up with a display that show-cases all the cultural and historical aspects of the country. Then you'll have to write a report on a certain time period in that country's history, and give a creative presentation to the class."

"Is the United States one of the countries?" Alex called out. "Because then baseball would def-initely be on the poster."

I had to hand it to Alex — he was seriously obsessed with baseball.

"No," Mrs. Bloom said, only this time she had a smile on her face. "We'll be discussing countries different from our own."

Dylan raised her hand. "Can we pick our own groups?" she asked.

I smirked. It wouldn't be hard to figure out who Dylan wanted in her group.

Mrs. Bloom shook her head. "No, I'll be assigning the groups," she said. "But you will be able to list the order of your preferences. There will be four different countries: Brazil, Mexico, France, and Japan."

"The Japanese love baseball," Alex shouted out. "And the Yankees love Japanese pitchers. They just signed another one last week."

"Yes, that's true," Mrs. Bloom said. "But we're going to focus on other aspects of their culture, too. Please write down your preferences, and hand them to me by the end of class."

The classroom filled with whispers. Everyone wanted to work with their friends, so we all had to coordinate preferences. I knew that was silly, since Mrs. Bloom would probably separate the groups of friends, anyway. But it was worth a try.

"The group presentations will take place on Friday, March sixth," Mrs. Bloom said as she wrote the date on the board.

Seeing the day before my party in white chalk on the blackboard sent a chill down my spine. There was so much to do — for the party, and now for this big project! And February was the shortest month of the year. How was I going to get everything done in time?

Where was my party planner when I needed her?

I glanced over at Marty, who was chatting with Drew. I wished that she'd move to a foreign country for the next five weeks. Maybe even five years. I didn't want her spoiling my plans for the perfect party.

CHAPTER FOUR

I didn't have time for a full-out pity party about Marty and Drew, or time to stress over whether any of the Royal Trio would be in my project group. A professional doesn't let things like that get in the way of planning a party.

When I got home from school that day, I had to switch into party-planning mode. The party was only four weeks and four days away!

I flipped open my purple notebook and reread an article about choosing the right invitations. "The invite is the guest's first impression of the party" — and I wanted that impression to be perfect.

"Carly! Time to go!" my mom called up the stairs.

Usually, when my mom and I go someplace, we get in the car and put on the radio right away. But Mrs. Dawson lived down the street, so we were walking over to talk to her about invitations. With no music playing, there was a whole lot of space for talk. But the invite list conversation was still fresh in my mind. Between that and Marty crushing on the same boy that I liked, I was in no mood to talk to my mom.

"How was school today?" my mom asked cheerfully as we walked out the door.

"Fine," I answered. I kicked a small pebble across the sidewalk, lodging it in a small crack in the pavement.

A red minivan drove down the street, and I watched it with great interest. It turned left at the corner, and then the street was bare.

"Did you think about the invitation list?" my mom asked as we walked across the street.

Was she serious? Had I thought about the list? It was *all* I could think about!

I kept my mouth shut.

When I didn't respond, my mom turned to face me. She raised her eyebrows and gave me a look.

"What?" I said, even though I didn't need any words to explain *that* look.

"Carly Ann," she said sternly. "You need to watch your attitude. The list needs to be cut."

"Fine," I replied. "I heard you." I stuck my hands deep in my jacket pockets and followed her up Mrs. Dawson's driveway.

Mrs. Dawson greeted us at the front door with a huge hello. Her mouth was outlined in bright red lipstick, and she rushed toward me to give me a hug.

"I just can't believe that you're turning thirteen!" she burst out as if she were singing a song from some Broadway show. Before my mom or I had a chance to respond, she ushered us downstairs to her office. "I remember when you were just a little baby!" she cried on the way. She shook her head slowly. "Where does the time go?"

The Dawsons' house smelled like chicken soup. My nose twitched as I stepped on the dark brown shag carpet covering the basement stairs. I tried to smile politely.

There were a round table and a couple of chairs in the center of the room. My mom and I sat down as Mrs. Dawson pulled a couple of binders off of a nearby shelf. "Let's start with these," she said, smiling.

I wondered if she could tell that I wasn't speaking to my mom. I shifted in the hard, wooden chair. Even though it was really hot and stuffy in the basement, I kept my jacket on.

"I love the idea of a candy theme," Mrs. Dawson said cheerfully. She sat down and flipped through one of the binders.

I couldn't help noticing Mrs. Dawson's long, shiny red nails, and the way that she carefully thumbed through the pages.

"That's a very clever, and original, theme," she went on. "We should be able to find a perfect invitation." She looked up at me and smiled.

I wondered if she kept talking to fill the silence between me and my mom.

"Ah, here it is!" Mrs. Dawson exclaimed. "This is the one I was looking for." She turned the binder around to show me.

The invitation looked like a candy dish with a lid. There were jelly beans, red licorice wheels, and other candy around the border of the paper. The words in the center were written in bright purple.

"Doesn't that just look delicious?" Mrs. Dawson said.

"Can we write 'Carly's Sweet 13' across the top?" I asked.

"Yes, of course!" Mrs. Dawson cried. "I think

that would look just darling." She turned to my mom. "What do you think, Marla?"

I watched my mom carefully. I really wasn't feeling up to another argument. Maybe because Mrs. Dawson was asking her, she'd agree that the invitation was perfect?

"Adorable," she replied after a pause. Then she turned to me. "You really like it, Carly?"

I nodded.

"Fantastic!" Mrs. Dawson said, placing an order form on the table. "How many would you like?"

I watched a crease appear between my mom's eyes. She glanced over at me, then turned back to Mrs. Dawson with a smile on her face.

"You know, I'll have to call you about that," she said evenly. "We're still ironing out the guest list."

Mrs. Dawson nodded. "I see," she said. "I'll just need to know within the next couple of days."

"We'll work on the list tonight. Right, Carly?" My mom looked at me intently.

"Yes," I replied, very aware that Mrs. Dawson was staring at me, too. Talk about pressure!

When we got home a few minutes later, my mom spread out my invite list on the counter.

"Carly, you need to cut some people. I'm serious about this."

I didn't mean to make a face, but hearing such sour news made me grimace.

"Don't make faces, Carly," my mother warned. "Just cut. Or I will." She put her arm around me and gave me a gentle squeeze. "You'll figure this out. It's going to be a great party."

I flopped my head into my hands. I wasn't so sure.

I picked up my purple pen and stared at the list of names. I tried to tackle the task as if it were a multiple-choice quiz. I would do the easy answers first, and skip over the names that I knew would stay.

But then I didn't cut anyone.

My cell phone rang, and I have to admit, I welcomed the distraction.

"Hey, Alex," I said, noting his name on my screen before I answered.

"What are you up to?" he asked.

"Trying to cut the party guest list," I groaned. "*Mom*zilla is roaring."

"Sounds like fun," Alex teased. "How's it going?"

I tapped my pen on the paper. "Not very well," I told him. "Any suggestions?"

"I don't know," he said. "Tough call. You want a big party, but you won't have a party at all if you don't cut the list down, right?"

He had a point. I knew better than to push my mom too hard. Her roar was loud, but she could do even more damage if I didn't do as she asked. "You're right," I said. "I just need to do it. Thanks, Alex."

"Yeah, no problem," he said. "Good luck."

"Thanks," I replied. "I'll need it." I hung up the phone and tossed it back in my bag.

With a heavy heart, I picked up my pen again and started to cross names off the list.

After dinner, when I brought my dishes into the kitchen, I noticed the list was still on the counter. Only I didn't see just my purple marks. There were some green markings on the page, too. I picked up the paper to have a better look.

My jaw fell open. I turned around to where my mom was standing at the sink.

"Martha Richards?" I said, my voice shaking. "You put *Martha Richards* on this list?"

There's a scene in the ballet *Sleeping Beauty*, where a wicked fairy, Carabosse, puts the baby princess Aurora under a sleeping spell. She's angry because she wasn't invited to the ball to celebrate the baby's birth. She dances as if she's a raging, red-hot fire-breathing dragon. The first time I saw the ballet, I was scared of that ballerina. I hid in my dad's coat the whole time she was onstage.

But right at that moment in the kitchen, I understood exactly where that fairy was coming from. Anger can change a person. My skin tingled with heat.

"You added Martha?" I asked through clenched teeth.

"Yes," my mom said calmly as if I was simply asking her if she had eaten dinner. She put a plate in the dishwasher and turned to face me. "There's no reason for you to get so upset. Your father and I only added a few people to the list."

I scanned the paper. Grandma and Grandpa, Aunt Jane and her new husband, and my parents' friends the Gottliebs and Richardses were all fine . . . but *Martha* Richards?

"Mom!" I cried. My hands curled into tight fists.

How could she do that to me? Martha Richards? Also known as — since the beginning of fourth grade — MARTY Richards!

"You know that Dale and Ken are good friends

of ours," my mother stated. "How can we have a party and not invite their family? They've known you since you were a baby!"

After I had spent the whole afternoon figuring out what names to cut, my mom went and added more? Not to mention that one of them was someone I couldn't stand!

"I know that you aren't friends with Marty anymore," my mom said, putting her arm around me. "But you used to be."

"A very long time ago," I corrected her.

"Fourth grade wasn't that long ago," she said.

"It was *forever* ago," I said. It might as well have been.

Fourth grade was not my favorite year. During the summer before fourth grade, our old dog, Slider, died. Plus, right before school started, Marty decided that she'd rather be Jordyn and Dylan's friend than mine or Lara's. She had a complete makeover that summer, worthy of a magazine spread. She went off to camp as Martha and came back as Jordyn's new BFF, Marty. They'd been in the same cabin at sleepaway camp, and had discovered that they were really BFF material. It was a complete — and completely awful — transformation.

Lara and I were shocked. After all, the three of us had all been best friends since nursery school. The first day of fourth grade, Martha showed up wearing pink lip gloss just like Jordyn and Dylan, and told everyone to call her Marty.

That was the end of Martha.

And the end of our friendship.

Marty was a different person. A person who didn't want to be friends with us.

Lara took the whole thing much better than I did. I'm not a big fan of change. And I didn't handle losing a best friend very well.

As if all that weren't enough of a reason to leave Marty off the guest list, I didn't want to invite competition to my own party. If Marty was crushing on Drew, inviting her was just asking for trouble. And I definitely didn't want trouble at my Sweet 13.

"She's going to ruin everything!" I cried. And I meant it.

Just then, my dad walked into the kitchen. "Carly," he said sternly. "That is not a very nice thing to say."

"Well, she's not the nicest person on the planet," I retorted. "And I don't want her at my party. Mom made me cut people I *like* from the list! For what? So I can have someone who hates me at my party?"

"Oh, I can't believe that Martha hates you," my mom said.

"Well, it's mutual," I grumbled.

Marty would probably attach herself to Drew at the party, and I would never get to dance with him. Or worse, maybe she'd be like Carabosse and put a wicked curse on the party! I knew I was getting carried away, but I didn't want any negative energy there. My nails dug into my palms as I squeezed my fists tighter.

"Maybe Marty doesn't want to come to your party," Olivia said, wandering into the kitchen. She sat down at the counter.

We all looked over at Olivia. She had a point — a good point.

"Oh, I don't think so," my dad said, shaking his head. "If I know Dale and Ken, they'll make sure that she comes."

I leaped up and grabbed my dad's hands. "Please, please encourage them to make Marty happy," I pleaded. "If she doesn't want to come, that's fine by me. More than fine!"

I could only hope that Olivia was right. I imagined Marty opening the invitation and sulking. She'd purse her lip-glossed mouth in a pout and complain that she didn't want to go to my silly, lame party.

"Carly," my mother said, snapping me out of it. "I don't like this behavior. You'd better watch your attitude."

Me? I wanted to cry out. Marty was the mean one! I couldn't control if Marty was in my class or even in my project group, but I should be able to control whether or not she was invited to my own birthday party!

My dad reached across the counter for a bag of cookies. "Ah, teenagers," he moaned.

"I think this is just the beginning of the drama," my mom mumbled.

"You mean horror show," my dad added, grinning. He came over and gave me a tight squeeze.

"Dad," I grumbled, annoyed that he was making jokes at a time like this.

"I remember when your aunt Jane turned thirteen, she became a *teen*zilla," my dad said. "You know, like the Godzilla movie that's playing in town." He laughed at his own joke. "Let's try to keep the monsters at the movies and not here at home, shall we?"

"Very funny," I said, sulking.

I was starting to wonder who the real monster was. After all, this was supposed to be *my* party! *Mom*zilla seemed to be squashing all my ideas.

But I wasn't going down without a fight.

CHAPTER FIVE

"Definitely get the chocolate chip cookies," Lara called to me as she pushed her lunch tray along the cafeteria line. "I'll grab our drinks."

I spotted the cookie platter up ahead and reached for three of them. "Got them!" I told her.

Frank, the Jefferson Middle School cook, liked to offer healthy food choices in the cafeteria. But every Tuesday he made a batch of his chocolate chip cookies. It would be a horrible understatement to say that we were thankful. The cookies were so popular that they disappeared quickly, so you had to get to lunch early to snag one.

Today, I really needed that cookie. I had already declared an emergency lunch meeting with Lara and Becca about the Marty-*monstrous* party disaster!

Lara swung her tray around the corner to the cash register. "Where's Becca?" she asked as she caught up to me.

"She's at the sandwich counter," I said, nodding toward the other side of the kitchen.

Becca was standing in front of the counter, instructing the lunch lady about how to create the perfect turkey sandwich. Becca was very particular about her food. She liked mustard, but only if it was spread directly on her turkey — not on the bread. I had to hand it to her, she did get the lunch lady to make a perfect Becca-wich every time.

"I can't believe your parents would do this to you," Lara said as we made our way to a table. "It's your party! You should invite who *you* want."

"Exactly," I said. "And they made it seem like I was being mean about it. How unfair is that?"

"Very," Lara agreed.

We headed for our usual table in the back of the cafeteria. On the way, we passed a table where a bunch of boys from our class were sitting. I couldn't help noticing that Drew was sitting with Ryan and the rest of the soccer team. He was even wearing the same green jersey as Ryan! I felt my stomach drop. Drew was friends with the popular boys, so why would he ever choose popular Marty over me? I looked down at my lunch tray as we walked by their table.

"What do you think Marty will do?" Lara asked. She slid into a bright orange cafeteria chair and flung her giant bag onto the seat next to her.

I sat down heavily and sighed. I wasn't sure. I poked at the mound of macaroni and cheese on my plate.

Becca put her tray down next to mine. "There's *no way* she's going to want to go to your party," she said emphatically.

"Thanks a lot," I said. I couldn't help but be a little hurt by the way that Becca put it. Even though I wished it were true!

"I don't mean it in a bad way," Becca added, smiling. "But think about it. Maybe Marty's not going to *want* to come."

"Her parents are going to make her go," Lara stated. She opened her yogurt and scooped up a spoonful. "They'll say that since she was invited, she needs to go. Her parents are totally into being proper. They're really nice . . . not like their daughter." Lara shrugged. "I spent a lot of time in that house, back when the doctor was around."

"The doctor" was code for the Martha Days —

MD. Since MD meant medical degree, that was how Lara and I referred to the time when we were friends with Martha. In fourth grade, we never wanted to say Martha's name, so I came up with a code word. Sometimes it still came in handy.

"Maybe you should call her parents. You could explain that it's fine with you if they don't come," Becca said around a mouthful of turkey and cheese.

"Very funny," I told her. I had a feeling that this meeting was going to have zero results.

"Let's stop talking about Marty," Becca said, making a face. "Let's talk about more important things . . . like your dress! Have you thought about what you're going to wear to the party?"

"A little," I confessed.

"You should get something totally sophisticated," Lara said, with a dreamy look on her face. "A real teenager dress."

"Whatever that means," Becca teased, rolling her eyes.

"I'll show you," Lara said. "Give me some paper."

Not only was Lara a shopper and a fashionista, she was also a budding designer. She was great at drawing clothes, and wanted to design her own one day.

I handed her my party-planning notebook and watched her draw a minidress with high-heeled boots. The girl in the picture looked very cool and sophisticated.

And *I* looked nothing like the girl!

"There's no way my mom would ever let me wear those boots," I said, shaking my head. "And I doubt that I could dance in those, let alone walk!"

We all giggled and started adding accessories to Lara's drawing.

Laughing at my addition of a hat with a feather, I looked up and saw Marty, Dylan, and Jordyn. They were walking over to a table near ours, at the back of the cafeteria. Their outfits coordinated, as usual — and they had matching lunches on their trays, too! There was no missing the sour look on Marty's face even from far away, but when she passed Drew's table, she plastered on a huge grin. I couldn't see Drew's reaction, but I could just imagine that he was happy to have one of those girls smile at him.

I stabbed my mac and cheese with my fork. "I wish I could have invited someone who I actually *like* to come to the party instead of her." I gritted my teeth and looked over at the next table, where Alyssa and Zoe were sitting. They both caught my eye and smiled. Knowing that I'd had to cut them from the list made my insides knot up. Those girls were so nice, *and* they didn't have crushes on Drew!

"Marty will probably be dancing with Ryan or Drew for the whole party," Becca said, shaking her head.

A piece of macaroni got stuck in my throat. I gagged and looked up at my friends. I felt big red blotches blossom on my cheeks.

"Did you really think we didn't know that you have a huge crush on Drew?" Becca asked, smiling slyly. "What kind of best friends do you think we are?"

I looked down at my tray, mortified! If they could tell, did anyone else know?

"Yeah, you're embarrassed, I know," Becca said. She put her hand on my arm. "But don't worry. He likes you, too."

"Becca!" I squealed.

I couldn't believe that she'd said that out loud — and Drew was eating his lunch nearby! I looked around frantically to see if anyone had overheard, but I seemed to be the only one freaking out.

"What did you do?" I whispered, leaning over to Becca. "Did you tell Drew that I had a crush on him? Becca!" I pushed my lunch tray away.

Suddenly, I wasn't hungry anymore. I felt light-headed. I felt weak.

Do people ever really die from embarrassment?

"No, I didn't *ask* him," she said casually. She picked up her sandwich. "I can just tell. I do have a sixth sense about these kinds of things, you know." She took a bite, as if everything was perfectly normal.

"Becca is usually right about people," Lara chimed in. "Remember, she knew that Greg was going to come and ask her to dance at his party?"

"He was dancing with *every* girl at his party," I replied. "She doesn't have a sixth sense."

"Oh, but I do," Becca said, grinning.

I wanted to believe that Becca knew something about Drew. Maybe she really did have a sixth sense about boys. And maybe jelly beans grew on trees.

Just then, Drew, Greg, and Ryan walked by our table. They were goofing around, laughing.

"Hey, Greg," Becca called, grinning.

Greg tapped Becca on the head as if we were playing a game of Duck, Duck, Goose. He moved on quickly with the pack of boys, heading toward the courtyard doors.

And then it happened.

Drew looked right at me — and smiled. Just when I thought my cheeks couldn't get any redder, they did!

And then in a flash, the boys were out the door.

"Now can you at least admit that I know what I'm talking about?" Becca gloated. She waved her sandwich in the air. "He totally looked right at you and smiled!"

"He did," Lara confirmed. "*Now* who cares if Marty comes to your party? You'll be dancing with Drew!"

I had to admit, I liked the sound of that.

That afternoon, I had gym. I don't mind gym when we can go outside and play on the field. Unlike some of the girls in my grade (named Marty, Jordyn, and Dylan), I like gym. But I'm not a huge fan of the Jefferson Middle School gymnasium. During the winter when it's cold, we have to use the gymnasium, which gets a little . . . stinky. To put it mildly.

Alex has these terrible allergies to mold. Once, he walked into the stinky gym and had a complete allergy attack. His eyes got puffy and red, and he was wheezing all over the place. Since then, they've tried all kinds of disinfectants to make the place smell better. But I think it's even worse.

Mr. Wu, our gym teacher, doesn't seem to like the indoor activities either. That afternoon, he was standing in the middle of the gym, trying to quiet the class. This was no easy task. There were two seventh grade classes in the gym, and everyone was talking.

Mr. Wu blew his whistle. "We'll be playing volleyball today," he called out, twirling the whistle around his finger like a lifeguard at the beach. "Listen up to the teams. There are four courts set up around the gym. Let's have the first group grab a pinny from the basket and head to the far court by the doors."

While he called out the teams, I ruminated about how much I hated those pinnies. They were made of neon orange nylon and smelled like old socks. Wasn't it bad enough wearing brown shirts and mustard-colored shorts? Whoever came up with the school colors for Jefferson Middle School didn't have the greatest fashion sense. Even I could have come up with a better combination. What about blue and white? Black and red?

Ms. Gator, the assistant gym teacher, motioned me over to the server's space on the court. I was the last one to arrive.

"Serve it up," Alex said, smiling at me from up near the net. He pulled on the visor of his baseball cap. (Gym was the only class where he was allowed to wear his hat.) I smiled back, happy to see a friendly face.

I got into position and quickly scanned the court. How'd I get so lucky to have Marty, Jordyn, *and* Dylan on my team? Sheesh.

Ms. Gator tossed me the ball, and I hugged it close. I actually like volleyball. I'm pretty good at it. And right at that moment, I felt like hitting the ball hard.

"Don't mess up," Jordyn sneered.

"If you can help it," Marty added under her breath.

I glared at them, then shifted my focus to the white ball. It was easy to imagine that the ball was Marty's head ... and I took great pleasure in whacking it very hard.

The ball sailed over the net, right to Greg's fingertips on the other side. He swiftly bumped it, aiming the ball for Marty, who was standing up at the net on our side. But instead of setting up her hands to hit the ball, she ducked. Then she popped her hip out and crossed her arms.

"Greeeeeg!" she sang out, smiling flirtatiously.

As if he'd aimed the ball at her because he wanted to ask her out — not to score the easiest point in the world for his team!

Greg laughed and gave Max a high five. "Our ball!" he cried.

In the meantime, Dylan and Jordyn rushed over to Marty.

"Are you all right?" Jordyn asked.

"That was a foul, Mr. Wu!" Dylan exclaimed.

Were they for real? I couldn't believe how ridiculous these girls were being. This was volleyball, where the game entailed hitting a ball back and forth. How did they not get that?

"Girls, please," Mr. Wu said, "Let's stay focused. Remember, hands up. Tap the ball up. Two taps, and over the net. Just like we did in the drills last week."

I shook my head as I moved to my next position on the court. Could I really like the same boy as Marty? We couldn't be more different! Then again, we were once exactly the same. When we were younger, she loved Fairytopia just as much as I did. We did everything together! But after her summer transformation, all that history was erased. She was more interested in being popular than being my friend.

I looked over at Nina Norwicki as she served the ball. She'd been in my class since fifth grade. We were in the school play together last year, and had fun rehearsing lines. I didn't have her on my speed dial or anything, but I liked her. I was sorry that I had crossed her name off the party list in the final cut. How come all the people I cut seemed to be the ones I liked the most today?

"One serving zero," Nina called out from across the net.

Exactly, I thought. With the way my day was going, I felt like a giant zero.

CHAPTER SIX

"Check this out," Lara said, pulling out a stack of catalogs from her book bag. She spread the glossy magazines out on Becca's bed. "Last night I went through all my catalogs," she explained, "and I picked out a few dresses that I thought would be good for your party."

We were supposed to be doing our homework at Becca's house, but researching a dress for my party seemed like the most important task at the moment.

"You didn't approve of the design from yesterday?" Becca asked, grinning at me. She flipped through the pages of the magazine closest to her. "Oh, this is a cute one!" she said, pointing to a black tank dress. "Totally A-list."

Lara flipped to a different page. "Now, this is the dress for you," she stated proudly. "What do you think?"

I looked down at the dress that she was pointing to. It was a light purple dress, with tiny spaghetti straps and silver and dark purple sequins. It was perfect. But scanning the page, I noticed the price of the dress in the corner.

"Um, I highly doubt that my mom would go for that," I said. But I couldn't help taking another look at the dress. I did need to get something extra special. And I did want to look good. A girl doesn't turn thirteen every day, after all.

"Can I borrow this catalog?" I asked.

Lara smiled. "Of course," she said. She turned to Becca. "See, I told you she would like it."

I stared at the girl in the photograph. She was dancing with a cute boy, and they looked like they were having a fantastic time. I couldn't help imagining dancing with Drew at my party. We'd be in the middle of the dance floor, and I'd be twirling around on new high-heeled shoes, wearing a beautiful, sparkly new dress.

Then I realized something.

"I can't wear high heels!" I blurted out.

"We'll help you. You can practice walking in them before the party," Lara said encouragingly.

But that wasn't the problem. "If I wear heels, I'll be taller than Drew!"

"So what?" Becca said, shrugging. "When I wear my shoes, I'll be taller than Greg."

"Plus, you'll take your shoes off when you dance, anyway," Lara said, trying to be helpful.

I shook my head and examined the model's shoes more closely. "I'd break my neck if I wore those," I said.

"How is it that you can walk across the balance beam perfectly in gym, but you can't wear heels?" Lara asked, wrinkling her nose at me. "For someone so athletic, you're a total klutz. You *have* to wear heels to your thirteenth birthday party!"

"We'll see," I said. I stood up and looked in Becca's mirror. "How do you think I should wear my hair at the party?" I asked, staring at my reflection.

"Definitely down," Becca said, sitting on the edge of the bed. "You look more sophisticated that way."

"For Aunt Jane's wedding, I had my hair up in a French twist," I said, gazing into the mirror. "I might do that. I'm not sure." I dropped my hair and it fell around my shoulders.

In the reflection, I saw Becca and Lara smiling at each other behind me. "What?" I asked, feeling self-conscious. "What are you looking at?" When they didn't answer, I turned to face them with my hands on my hips.

"Let's give it to her now," Lara said. Her blue eyes were shining brightly.

"Wait here," Becca instructed me. "We'll be right back."

They both ran out of the room, giggling. I felt a little funny, standing in Becca's room alone in front of the mirror. I had spent a lot of time in her room, but still, it was awfully quiet. Just when I started to get weirded out, my friends came barreling back in through the door.

"Okay," Lara said, handing me a small box. "This is part of your birthday present. We thought that you'd like to have it early."

"Aw," I cooed. My first birthday present! I grinned at my two best friends. "Thank you."

"Wait — open it before you thank us!" Becca said, smiling.

I carefully pulled off the purple bow and tied it in my hair, then unwrapped the glittery pink paper. There was a little tan box inside.

"Go on," Lara said. "Open it already!"

I lifted the lid to see a dazzling silver tiara. It even had little hearts and stars on it. It was beautiful!

"Try it on!" Becca cried. "We thought you'd want to wear something special in your hair for the party."

"We spent a long time searching," Lara explained. "But we definitely got the right one!"

I reached out to hug my friends. The gift was not only perfect, it was so thoughtful, too. I had the best friends. "I love it!" I slipped the tiara on my head, feeling extra-special already.

"You look like a princess," Lara sighed.

"A movie star," Becca chimed in.

"A teenager?" I asked, smiling.

My friends laughed and crushed me in a hug.

"I can't wait for my big dance-floor moment," I confessed, sitting down on the bed next to my friends. "You know, when two people meet on the dance floor for that special dance . . ."

"You are such a sap!" Becca cried, flinging a pillow at my head. "Was that in some movie or something?"

"It's in just about every movie!" Lara said. "And Carly should know — I think she owns every romantic comedy ever made."

"I'm serious," I told them. I turned back to the mirror and straightened the tiara on my head. "I want that moment."

"We really should do our homework," Becca

said, pulling out her notebook. "My mom will yell at me if I don't finish. I have a piano lesson in an hour."

"Did you start on your social studies project?" Lara asked me as she unpacked her notebook from her humongous bag. "I can't believe Drew and Greg are both in your group."

"And don't forget that Marty is, too," I said, flipping open my math book. "We have research time next week in the library, so hopefully we'll get something done. But I'm afraid we're not going to learn much about Mexico. I have a feeling it's going to be the Marty Show."

"A *horror* show," Becca said, laughing.

"Don't remind me," I said. "You two are so lucky that you're together in the France group."

"*Oui,*" they both said at the same time, giggling.

I threw a pillow at each of them.

At first, I was really excited about researching Mexico. I didn't know much about it, but everything I knew seemed ultracool. But from the moment Mrs. Bloom read the group list to the class, I knew I was in trouble.

I'd gotten to work on the country that I wanted, but there was one little problem: Marty.

Why did Mrs. Bloom have to put her in my group? As hard as I tried, I couldn't get away from her! But I couldn't be too angry with Mrs. Bloom. She'd also put me in the same group as Drew.

I settled in on Becca's floor and did my math assignment. Thinking about numbers for the next twenty minutes would be a welcome break.

When I got home from Becca's house, there was a large box on the kitchen table.

"I waited for you to open it," my mom said, smiling.

I checked out the label. "My invitations!" I cried as I ripped open the seal.

There were two white boxes buried inside the shipping carton. One had the 'invitations, and the other had the bright purple envelopes. Finally seeing the invitations made everything so real. I was actually going to have a super Sweet 13 party!

"Wow," Olivia said, peering into the box and pulling out an invitation. "That is so cute!"

"Not cute," my mom corrected her. "Cool." She gave me a hug. "Do you like them, Carly?"

"I do!" I cried. "They're perfect."

"Where'd you get the tiara?" Olivia asked, staring at my head.

"Becca and Lara gave it to me," I said, twirling so the tiara would catch the light. "Isn't it great?"

"And very shiny," my mom added.

"I'm wearing it for the party," I told her.

My mom nodded as she organized the kitchen table. "Let's get these invitations in the mail! Olivia, if you don't mind stuffing the invites into the envelopes, I'll stamp them, and Carly can write the addresses."

Working together, we finished up the task pretty quickly. (Though my hand was throbbing after addressing all those envelopes.) When we were finished, I ran to my bag, grabbed the page from Lara's catalog, and smoothed it out.

"This is the dress I found for the party," I said. I slid down into a chair next to my mom.

"Wow," she said. "That's quite the dress."

"Don't you love it?" I asked.

My mom raised her eyebrows and sighed. "Well, it is pretty, but this is a very expensive dress."

I was hoping my mom wouldn't look at the bottom corner of the page, where the price was listed. Too late. "But Mom," I pleaded, "I need to wear something fancy. This dress would be perfect for me."

"Carly," she said, looking me straight in the eye. "This dress costs too much."

How could my mom not understand? I *needed* that dress. I wanted to be that beautiful girl, dancing with a cute boy — a cute boy named Drew. "I have some allowance money," I said.

"Not that much," my mom said, shaking her head. "I'm sure we can find something else that will be just as nice. How about we go to the mall after we drop Olivia at ballet?"

"Oh, can't I go, too?" Olivia cried.

My mom put the completed envelopes in a tall pile. "No, you have your ballet lesson," she said.

Olivia pouted, but I couldn't help grinning. Even though I was annoyed that my mom had vetoed the dress in the catalog, I knew that nothing made Olivia madder than being left out of a shopping trip. I could consider it revenge for all the mornings she'd hogged the bathroom.

My mom and I dropped Olivia off at her ballet class and headed to the mall. I was ready for a serious search-and-find mission.

Our first stop was Jessica's Closet, a boutique store for teens at the mall. I loved their clothes — there were tons of cute dresses to choose from!

"Hello, my name is Audrey," a saleswoman

said, walking over to us. "Are you looking for anything special this afternoon?"

"Yes," I replied, standing up straighter. "I'm shopping for a dress for my thirteenth birthday party."

Audrey smiled. "Oh, we have several new special occasion dresses." She led us to the back corner of the store. "Look through these racks here," she said, gesturing. Then she turned to face me. "Do you know what kind of style that you're looking for?"

I wasn't really sure how to answer that question. As much as I wanted to look glamorous for the party, I wasn't the fashionista that Lara was — not by a long shot. So I just smiled. "Something special," I replied simply.

"Well, that should be easy enough," Audrey said. She pulled out a bright lemon-colored dress with a flower print.

I shook my head no. I didn't like yellow — or big orange flowers!

"Carly, what about this?" my mom asked.

I looked over at her . . . and gasped. Was she kidding? The dress she was holding was white with a pink satin ribbon around the center. It was a dress that a three-year-old might wear, not a thirteen-year-old!

"Mom!" I cried. "No way."

My mother grinned and held up her hands, surrendering. "Okay, okay," she said, sliding the dress back on the rack. "How about this?"

This time, the dress she pulled was pink lace with tiny white buttons down the front. I couldn't help wondering if it came with a matching bonnet. What was she thinking?

"This looks like a piece of candy, doesn't it?" my mom asked, smiling. "Isn't it just darling?"

Maybe for a baby, I wanted to say. But I didn't say anything. I just shook my head and turned to focus on the rack in front of me. While I wasn't sure what style I wanted, I was *very* sure what style I *didn't* want. If this was my first night as an official teenager, I wasn't going to spend it wearing a baby dress.

"How about this one?" I said a few minutes later, pulling out a deep purple strapless dress. It was the color of my favorite jelly bean, Purple Passion. There was a thin row of dark purple sequins around the waist, and a thicker band of sequins at the bottom. I held the dress up in front of me. The length was perfect — just above my knees.

My mom's eyes popped open. "Absolutely not," she said, turning back to the rack in front

71

of her without another word. She continued pushing one dress at a time off to the side. The clinking of the hangers on the silver bar echoed in the air.

"I didn't even try it on," I argued. "You always say that I need to try things on! Don't you want to see how the dress looks before you veto it?"

My mother pursed her lips. "You are not wearing a strapless dress, Carly."

"Why not?" I asked. I held the dress up, admiring it. "It's less expensive than the other dress I liked," I said, appealing to my mom's thrifty side. I loved the color, and the material was super soft. Plus, I had never worn a strapless dress before. Marty had worn one to Mindy's party — what if she wore one to mine? I didn't want her to look fancier than me.

"It's not appropriate," my mom said. "This is your thirteenth birthday party, not your sixteenth."

I rolled my eyes. "Come on, Mom," I wheedled. "Let me just try it on. You always say that I look great in purple, right?"

"Purple is a good color for you," my mom conceded. "But Carly, you are not wearing a strapless dress."

"All the girls love that dress," Audrey said, walking over to us. "It's a very easy dress to wear, and very affordable." She smiled at me.

I knew I'd liked her from the moment I saw her.

"No," my mom said. This time she didn't even look up from the rack.

Tears started to well up in my eyes. Oh, boy. I knew that if I started to cry, I wouldn't be able to stop. My mom always tells the story about a tantrum that I had in a department store when I was two years old. I hid in the clothing rack for more than an hour, screaming at the top of my lungs. She was mortified, and had to crawl into the rack to drag me out. I don't remember that day, but at this moment I kind of wanted to just start screaming.

"Carly," my mom said in a low voice, trying to avoid making a scene. "I really don't think you'll even be comfortable in a strapless dress."

"But I've never even tried one on," I said. A tear slid out of my eye, and I quickly wiped it away. How was I going to be a teenager if I couldn't stop crying like a baby?

"Go try it on," my mom said, sighing. I saw her catch Audrey's eye. They seemed to share a moment of understanding . . . which made me want to scream all over again.

I ducked behind the heavy red dressing room curtain and slipped the dress on. Then I stared at myself in the three mirrors before me. The dress looked ridiculous! Instead of making me look sophisticated and older, it made me look like a little kid in dress-up clothes.

"Carly, are you going to come out and show us?" my mom called.

When I didn't answer, she poked her head inside the dressing room.

"Audrey found a similar outfit in a different style," she said. She moved the curtain to reveal the same color purple material in a tank top and matching purple miniskirt. There was a thin row of sequins along the neckline and a small satin bow on one side of the tank. My mom smiled at me. "Try it on," she said. "I think that this is going to fit you beautifully."

I took the hanger and slipped the outfit on. What a difference! I proudly stepped out of the dressing room and twirled around.

My mom beamed. "What do you think?"

"I found my outfit!" I said happily. I spun around, admiring the sequins in the mirror. Maybe it wasn't the dress I'd seen in the catalog, but it was beautiful. I turned to my mom. "Can I get high heels, too?"

"We can try on some shoes," she said. My mom was like a whole new person, now that we'd found an outfit we both agreed on. "I suppose you're ready for some heels."

Audrey brought out a pair of beautiful black patent leather shoes with thin, dainty heels for me to try on. When I put them on, I felt totally glamorous. So what if Drew was going to be shorter than me? I looked amazing.

"They're perfect," I said.

"Carly, you really should walk around a little," my mom said. "See if they hurt your feet."

Now she was totally embarrassing me. I was old enough to know if shoes fit me or not! I didn't have to go parading around the store like a little kid. "I want these," I said firmly.

My mom checked the price on the box and sighed. "Okay," she said.

I glanced over at Audrey, who was smiling at me. "You're going to look beautiful. Have fun at the party," she said.

I had a feeling I would.

CHAPTER SEVEN

Friday morning at school marked three weeks until our group projects were due (and three weeks and one day until my party!). My group — me, Drew, Greg, Marty, Nina, and Alex — was scheduled to go to the library to do research. Normally, I would have welcomed the chance to get out of the classroom and go to the project room in the back of the library. The big conference table and chairs made it really comfortable. But considering who was in my group this time, I wasn't so sure about it.

"Hello," Mrs. Howard whispered to our group when we walked through the glass doors of the library. "I've pulled some books on Mexico for you to look through."

Mrs. Howard ran the school library as if it were a holy religious site. The library was renovated last year, so there were new tables, chairs, and carpeting. It was a cool place, and I loved going there. But Mrs. Howard was very strict about her rules. There was no talking above a whisper, no food allowed, and absolutely no joking around. She guarded the books as if they were precious treasures, and insisted that everyone follow her library etiquette. Unfortunately for me, she also played tennis with my mom on Wednesday nights, so I always felt as if she was watching me extra closely. Maybe it was just because she knew my name, but I tried to be on my best behavior whenever I was in the library. It couldn't hurt.

"Thank you," I said then. I smiled, trying to be the star student that I knew my mom wanted me to be. I was definitely doing my best, at school and at home, to stay on her good side before the party. I was trying not to fight with Olivia (as hard as that was) and doing all my chores.

Greg and Drew walked over to a nearby table and grabbed two books. They were goofing around a little, and Mrs. Howard gave them a stern look.

"Take a few books, and then you can head into the project room to talk," Mrs. Howard said, clipping her words.

We each grabbed some books and went to the project room. Nina was very serious and took about four books, while Marty just took one — the thinnest one on the table. Of course.

As soon as we all were in the room with the door closed behind us, Marty didn't need any prompting. She plopped down in a chair and started spouting orders.

"I think we should just start writing down ideas," she said. She tore a piece of paper from her notebook. I couldn't help noticing that her short blond hair was perfectly in place, and her blue shirt matched her eyes — a fact that I'm sure she was well aware of when she picked out the shirt.

"I have neat handwriting, so I can do the writing," Marty stated to no one in particular.

"Don't you think we should do some research first?" I asked. "There were a lot of books on the table. We should probably look at a few of them before we start."

"If you want," Marty said, shrugging as if she couldn't care less. She probably couldn't.

I quickly glanced around the table. "Did anyone take a book on Mexican music?" I asked. "That's a big part of Mexican culture."

When Aunt Jane and Uncle John went to Mexico for their honeymoon, they brought back maracas and a CD of really cool music. I wanted to research that aspect of Mexican culture myself.

"There was a book about music, but I think we left it up front," Drew said. "We should go get it." He stood and headed for the door.

I thought that my heart was going to leap right out of my chest. Did he just use the word *we* — as in, him and me?

I couldn't wipe the grin off my face as I followed him out the door. I could feel Marty's laser glare on my back as Drew and I left the room. But as soon as we got through the door, Greg raced up behind us.

"I'll come with you," he said.

Way to ruin the moment, Greg! I tried not to scowl. Why did he have to follow us?

"By the way," Greg whispered as we walked over to the display table. "Cool invitation for your birthday party."

"Yeah," Drew said.

My breath got caught in my throat and I couldn't respond.

"Sounds like it will be a great party," Greg added.

I stared at the little brown and beige squares on the library rug. I felt paralyzed. Was I really going to miss an opportunity to talk to Drew due to a temporary loss of speech? How lame!

"Um, thanks," I finally spat out. Not the greatest line ever mumbled, but at least I managed to say something.

"Shhh," Mrs. Howard scolded from her desk. Great.

My shoulders caved and I rushed over to the table with the Mexico books.

Alex came bouncing up behind us. "Check this book out," he said loudly. He held up a book titled *Mexico's Baseball Obsession*. "We should totally take this one."

"Shhhhhh," Mrs. Howard said from the front desk, a little more forcefully this time. "Please take the books back to the project room, where you can talk."

Alex nodded, scooped up two more books, and motioned for us to come with him. Since I didn't seem to have a voice to communicate with, I just followed the boys to the project room with the book about Mexican music in my hand.

When we got back to our seats, Nina was stationed in front of four open books. She was scribbling notes in her notebook while Marty applied lip gloss.

So much for Marty's good handwriting.

"We need a theme," Nina said. "You know, something to tie all this information together."

Good old Nina. I felt another pang of guilt for not inviting her to my party.

"And don't forget, we have to present it to the class, too," Alex added.

Drew's green eyes met mine, and I realized in horror that I must have been staring at him. I quickly looked down at the Mexican music book in my lap. I kept trying to think of a good idea to contribute to the discussion, but I was still feeling paralyzed.

"Let's do a poster like you'd see in a travel agency," Greg said. "You know, like a giant advertisement for the whole country."

Everyone turned to look at him.

"That's a great idea," I said, finally finding my voice. "We could show all the cool things about the country's culture."

Drew looked at me and smiled. "I love it."

If I were a chocolate candy, I would have melted. I suddenly had a newfound love for Mexico — the country that had brought me and Drew together!

"I love it, too," Marty said quickly. She gave me an icy look.

But even that couldn't ruin my good mood.

We spent the rest of the period figuring out what should go on the poster, and what topics everyone's essays would cover. Right before the end of the period, Mrs. Howard knocked on the door. "Your time is up," she whispered. "You'll need to check out the books that you want and head back to Mrs. Bloom's class."

We nodded, gathering up our books and notebooks. I couldn't help wondering if Mrs. Howard spoke in whispers when she got home.

I walked back to the room with Nina and Alex, behind Greg, Drew, and Marty. I didn't *mean* to listen in on their conversation. I know that eavesdropping is rude. But how could I not?

"The game was awesome," Greg said. "Drew was on fire! The goalie never stood a chance against his penalty kick."

"I wish that I could have seen the game," Marty cooed.

I stifled a groan. Could she be any more obvious? I tried to get a glimpse of Drew's reaction. Did he like her? I had to hand it to Marty — at least she was able to actually speak to Drew. I couldn't manage to say anything directly to him without stuttering. Not exactly a great way to let someone know you like him.

"So now we just have to win the next two games," Greg went on. "If we win, then we play in the finals. The championship game is being played at Greenville on March seventh. Hope we can pull it off."

I froze. March seventh?

"I'm sure you'll win," Marty said, batting her eyes.

"Isn't that the day of your party?" Alex whispered in my ear.

I shot him a stern look. Nina was right next to me. I didn't want to talk about the party in front of her, or let on that I was freaking out! If the soccer games went like Greg described, the boys would be playing an away game on the day of my party! Greenville was more than two hours away. What if the game was in the afternoon? What if none of the boys on the team was able to come? That would mean ten missing boys — and a totally uneven dance party.

The more I thought about my conversation with Drew in the library (if you could call it that), the more I realized that he never actually said he was planning on coming. None of the boys on the soccer team had responded yet. There was still time before the RSVP date, but . . . I tried to swallow my panic.

I wondered what an experienced party planner would say. I didn't have a real party planner to consult, but I knew I could count on the next best thing — Lara and Becca.

When we got back to the classroom, I stared at the large clock above Mrs. Bloom's door. The hands moved so slowly! I thought I might burst before I could talk to Lara and Becca.

The bell finally rang, and I rushed over to my best friends. I waited until the three of us were standing at our lockers to tell them what I had overheard.

"You don't know for sure that the boys will play on the seventh," Lara said, trying to reassure me.

"Don't worry," Becca added, searching for her notebook in her locker. "Don't panic yet."

It was hard not to.

If the boys didn't come to the party, everything would be ruined! The party wouldn't be a sweet success — it would be a sloppy, gooey mess.

After school, my mom, Olivia, and I went over to the Riverhouse to meet with Sylvia, the manager. I was still feeling anxious after overhearing

Greg's conversation that afternoon, but seeing the Riverhouse got me all excited for the party again.

When we walked in, Sylvia introduced me to the DJ, Myles. Myles looked as though he had just come from a runway photo shoot. He had dark, curly hair and deep blue eyes with long lashes. I couldn't wait for Becca and Lara to meet him. They were going to love him!

"Hey, there," Myles said. He had a deep voice that sounded like a radio announcer, and held out his hand for me to shake. "You must be the star of the Sweet 13 party that I've been hearing about."

My cheeks flared up instantly. "Uh, yes," I managed to say.

He winked at Olivia, then shook my mom's hand. "We're all looking forward to the party in a couple of weeks," he said. He handed me a piece of paper and a pen. "I have a sheet here for you to fill out. It's a checklist of songs that you might want to hear — or *not* hear — at the party."

"Great," I said. I definitely had opinions on that subject.

"How many dancers would you like at the party?" Myles asked.

What did he mean? I wanted everyone to dance!

When he saw the confused look on my face, he smiled. "We have dancers who come and motivate the crowd. They're all really talented. I usually suggest hiring about six for a party this size."

Oh, just like Kara had at her party! I thought, remembering the details I'd heard.

"Six?" my mom echoed. The familiar crease in her forehead was back.

"Sure, it keeps the party moving," Myles said. "And we can do some fun things, too, like carry Carly in for her entrance, create a cake ceremony, have Carly do a choreographed dance with the dancers...."

I envisioned a royal entrance, being carried by four dancers just like the queen of Sheba being welcomed by the court. There'd be a smoke machine, confetti, and lots of cheers. If all the dancers looked like Myles, I would feel like a total movie star on opening night.

Then my mom's voice broke into my daydream.

"I don't think we need all that," she said. "We're thinking more low-key."

I wanted to shout, *No, we're not!*

My party was definitely not supposed to be low-key. Was my mom purposely trying to sabotage the party? Momzilla was roaring, and I was ready to fight. We already battled over the invitation list and the dress, but now the entertainment?

No way!

"Mom," I said through gritted teeth.

"I understand," Myles told us. He looked over at me and smiled widely. "We're gonna have a blast, don't worry, Carly. Just e-mail me that list of songs, and we'll be sure to play your favorites. I bet your crowd doesn't need a whole lot of motivation to dance."

I hadn't really thought about that. At Mindy and Greg's party, it seemed as if most kids were dancing. But then again, there were almost triple the amount of kids at their party!

"And here's a packet of our menus for the party," Sylvia said, walking over to my mom. "We can finalize the menu once you get your head count set. Right now, we have some cake samples that we'd love for you to try," she said. "You can taste the samples, and let us know which you like best."

"Thanks," I said. I eyed the menus, and was happy to see that there were choices of lots of different kinds of food — and no pizza.

"The cake samples are in the back room. It's

set up for a party later tonight," Sylvia added. "It will give you a good idea of how the place looks all decorated."

My mom and Olivia followed me into the room. There were bunches of silver and white balloons on each of the small round tables, and glittering stars hung down from the ceiling.

"Tonight's party is to launch a new fragrance called Midnight, so we went with a nighttime sky theme," Sylvia explained. "We can do brightly colored balloons coming out of baskets of candy on your tables, if you'd like. The balloons make things festive."

At one table were four different pieces of cake. Olivia zoomed past me and sat down in one of the chairs. She picked up a fork and moved to attack the white cake with pink frosting.

"Hold up," I said, grabbing her hand. "I get first taste."

Olivia made a face and slunk back in her chair. I picked up a fork and dug into the dark chocolate cake with white icing.

"Is this marshmallow icing?" I asked Sylvia around my mouthful.

"Yes," she replied with a grin. "It's one of my favorites."

"Yum, and one of mine, too!" I said, licking my lips. I dug into the other pieces, and then Olivia and my mom tasted the cakes.

"Definitely the chocolate with the marshmallow," Olivia said.

My mom nodded. "I think that's my favorite, too."

I was glad that finally we all agreed on something!

"I was thinking we could have a long table here, with candy set up," Sylvia said, waving her hand toward the front of the room. "And Vito, our chef, does an amazing dessert table. A chocolate fountain, fondue, and these heavenly little homemade chocolates."

All I could think about was the surprised look on everyone's faces when they saw the sweet spread. The only time I ever saw a chocolate fountain was in a movie about a princess. The girl was at a royal ball, and there was a huge fountain of milk chocolate. She dipped strawberries and tiny marshmallows in it with a fancy silver stick.

"What about the ice-cream dessert we talked about earlier?" my mom asked.

"But it's a candy-themed party," I said. "A chocolate fountain would be perfect!"

Sylvia nodded. "The fountain *is* an added expense," she admitted. "We can do the ice-cream-cone cart and then have a table here with buckets of candy." She turned to look at me. "We have these darling silver buckets that would look fantastic all lined up. They'd give the candy theme a real boost."

I wanted to reach out and hug Sylvia. That sounded amazing. She was totally thinking like a member of Team Sweet 13!

"And what about a bubble machine?" I asked. "You know, for the dance floor?"

My mom peered up at the ceiling. I could tell that she was adding numbers in her head.

Sylvia smiled. "Yes, we have a bubble machine, and I'm sure Myles will find a time to shower you and your friends."

"Is that extra?" my mom asked.

"No," Sylvia said. "Bubbles are part of the package."

I looked around the Midnight room, imagining it filled with my friends, all admiring the colorful baskets of candy on the tables.

It seemed like things were finally looking up!

For now, anyway.

CHAPTER EIGHT

I know that there's some saying "patience is a virtue," but whoever said that must not have been waiting on responses to come back for a party.

It was exactly one week until my party, and the official RSVPs were all due by the end of the day. Still, I hadn't been able to check off the boxes next to Marty and the soccer team's names. The boys on the team would know the next day — Sunday — whether or not they were playing in the finals. But I hadn't heard from Marty at all. Typical. I knew that Marty's parents were coming, but their RSVP didn't include Marty's name. I was hoping that no news was good news.

No RSVP e-mail from Marty was driving me crazy . . . but then again, everything was driving me a little crazy.

In the two weeks before the party, I was trying to grow my nails, not bruise or skin my knees (especially during tennis lessons), and use deep conditioner on my hair. I wanted to look my best for the party! When Lara suggested a "spa night" sleepover on Saturday, I was all for it. Lara had gotten a Spa in a Box for Christmas, and we all agreed that a week before the party was the perfect time to break into the beauty treatments.

While we were waiting for Lara to mix up the seaweed vitamin-enriched nourishing mask, I logged on to her computer. I held my breath as I checked my e-mail. I love getting messages, and I especially loved getting responses to the party.

So I especially hated it when my empty mailbox popped up.

The thing about checking e-mail constantly is the depressing "no mail" moment. I turned away from the computer, feeling dejected.

"Did you know that in Mexican culture, girls have quinceañeras when they turn fifteen?" I asked Lara and Becca, trying to take my mind off the missing RSVPs. "Those are usually huge celebrations, and the parties are over the top."

"You definitely have parties on the brain," Lara said, rolling her eyes. She rubbed some cream on her elbows and passed the tube over to Becca.

"Well, of course I do," I said. "My party is only a week away!"

"So we've heard," Becca mumbled.

"There's a lot to do," I went on. I reached down for my notebook and scanned my checklist. "Did I tell you that I picked out the containers for the jelly beans?" I tapped my purple pen on my chin. "They're so cute! The guy at Candy World said we could tie purple ribbons on them that say, 'Carly's Sweet 13.' We ordered fifty pounds of jelly beans!"

"Uh-huh," Lara said absentmindedly. She poked at the green goop. "Let's do the face mask. The stuff is ready." She skillfully spread the mask over her face with a tiny paintbrush.

"It's like green slime!" Becca said, jumping off the bed. "I want some!"

"And in the center of each table there's going to be a basketful of candy with a bunch of rainbow-colored balloons tied to the top," I went on. "I told my mom that I wanted to donate the centerpieces to a children's hospital after the party, to share the candy with kids who would appreciate it."

"You told us that already," Becca said, peering into the mirror and spreading the green mixture over her face.

"We have to leave this on until it dries," Lara read off the Spa in a Box label. "Carly, try some."

I reached out for the brush of goopy green cream. "The big question is," I said as I applied the mask, "whether or not the boys on the soccer team can make it."

"I don't know if I can wait anymore," Becca said, sighing.

"I know," I sighed. "The suspense is killing me!"

Becca gave me a hard, long look. "I was talking about washing off my mask," she said.

Lara glanced over at the clock on her nightstand. Her blond hair was pulled up in a high ponytail on top of her head, and her face was electric green. "We just have to leave it on for a few more minutes," she advised.

I shook my head, feeling jittery. "I can't believe it — at this time next week we'll be at my party!" I said.

"Don't talk — you'll crack your mask," Lara scolded me.

"I don't think Carly can stop talking about her

party," Becca mumbled, trying not to move her stiff cheeks.

"What's that supposed to mean?" I asked.

"I guess it's been long enough," Lara broke in, heading into the bathroom. "Let's rinse."

We all filed into her bathroom to wash off the masks. I had to admit, goopy as it was, the Spa in a Box definitely made my face feel smoother.

"Lara, can I check my e-mail?" I asked, rinsing my washcloth in the sink.

Lara didn't look at me. "Let me guess — you want to check your party responses?"

"It's only been about ten minutes since you've looked," Becca grumbled.

They shared a look.

"What?" I said. I looked at them and shrugged. "Don't you want to know who's coming?"

"All you've talked about since you got here was your party," Lara spat, walking out of the bathroom.

I followed her, slid into her desk chair, and logged on to my e-mail account. "Very funny," I said.

But no one was laughing.

I forgot about that as soon as my inbox came up on the screen. I froze. "There's an e-mail from Marty!"

There was the reply that I had dreaded since I'd seen Marty's name scrawled in green pen on my invitation list. I quickly read the e-mail.

My heart sank.

"I can't believe it," I muttered. "She's actually going to come to the party!" I leaned forward and read the e-mail out loud. "'Carly, My parents said that I had to write and tell you that I'm coming to your party. — Marty.'"

"Why do you care so much if she comes?" Becca asked. "If you don't like her, what does it matter what she thinks?"

I turned around and glared at Becca. How could she even ask me that?

"Can we *please* talk about something else besides the party?" Lara sighed heavily and sat down on her pink beanbag in a huff.

I narrowed my eyes. "What did you just say?"

The room was completely silent.

"Is that how you really feel?" I prodded Lara.

"Lara," Becca said. It sounded as if she was warning her to beware of some ferocious dog or something.

When I realized that *I* was the scary dog, I turned my back to them both and took a deep breath. This was clearly some kind of misunderstanding.

"Come on," I said after a minute. "This is going to be the party of the year."

"Yeah, well, not *everything* this year needs to be about your party!" Becca snapped.

"I'm kinda tired of talking about your party," Lara chimed in quietly. "It's all we've been talking about for weeks."

I couldn't believe it. I couldn't believe *them*! "Wait, do you realize how much I've been planning for this? Do you have any idea about all the details and decisions that go into making a perfect party?" My voice was getting louder, but I couldn't stop. "I'm under a ton of pressure here. What kind of best friends are you?" I shouted.

The impact of my words didn't take long. Lara's eyes welled up fast, and Becca looked away.

"Just because you're turning thirteen doesn't mean you get to be such a beast!" Becca cried. Her face was flushed. "Remember when you said this party was for all of us? It doesn't feel like that anymore." She reached down and grabbed her backpack. "I'm going home."

Becca stormed out of the room.

I glanced up at the clock. It was only 7:30. "I guess the sleepover is over, huh?" I asked.

Lara shrugged. She didn't even look at me.

I picked up my backpack and headed for the

door. I had even brought the best "four heart" movies for later. I guessed I'd be watching those at home . . . alone.

I couldn't remember a time that I'd ever had a fight with Lara and Becca. As I stomped up the block to my house, I started to feel less angry and more sad. I had been so worried about Marty creating drama, but really, I'd created my own horror show.

Maybe Becca was right — maybe I was the one who'd turned into a monster.

CHAPTER NINE

One afternoon that week, I opened my party-planning notebook and stared at the calendar pasted in the middle. My birthday was coming on fast — and I wasn't feeling the party spirit.

Lara and Becca still weren't talking to me. I probably wasn't helping the situation by not talking to them, but I didn't know what to do. Since the sleepover at Lara's on Saturday night, everything had changed. Even when I heard that the boys' soccer game was going to be in the morning, and that they'd all be able to come to my party, I couldn't be 100 percent happy. The boys were going to be at my party ... but would Lara and Becca be there?

At least my Mexico project was going well. I

had burned a CD of lots of cool Mexican music, and made a chart of instruments that were popular in Mexican culture. Each member of our group was supposed to be doing one element of the poster, and we each had to write an essay about a different time period in Mexican history. Amazingly, everyone stuck to the plan we'd come up with that first day in the library.

My essay was about Mexico in the 1930s. Since I was in the middle of my own Great Depression, I was totally in the right frame of mind to be writing about Mexico during a depressed time in world history.

This was the week that I looked forward to all year, and now it was going by way too fast. I almost didn't want Friday to come! If my best friends didn't come to the party, I wasn't going to have a good time at all.

"Are you ready for the big presentation?" my dad asked when I walked into the kitchen Friday morning.

"I guess so." I shrugged.

"I'm sure your group is going to do well," my mom said, handing me a plate of scrambled eggs.

"When I'm in seventh grade, I'm going to be the star of my project group," Olivia sang out. "Don't you think?" She flashed me one of her huge smiles from across the table.

I wasn't in the mood.

"I don't doubt that for a minute," I said, wondering if she could sense my snide tone. It was hard to miss.

"How are Becca and Lara?" my dad asked. He poured coffee into his mug and sank a teaspoon of sugar into the dark brew. "I haven't seen them around all week."

I looked over at the mug that he was holding. Lara, Becca, and I had made our dads mugs for Father's Day last year. We had spent the day at Paint Now, a paint-your-own-pottery store at the mall. We all chose the same mug, but mine was a bit of a mess because I couldn't decide what color to use and wound up using three or four. It came out a lovely shade of . . . muddy brown. (Becca called it chocolate brown, not muddy brown — which I appreciated.) Lara made hers all yellow, and Becca drew three little cups around the mug and wrote her name and her two brothers' names under each cup. It had been such a fun day. My eyes started to well up, just looking at the mug.

"Oh, no," my dad said in a panic when he saw

my reaction. "What did I say?" He looked like a kid who'd broken his mother's favorite vase.

My mom came over and wrapped me in a hug. When I'd come home from Lara's house on Saturday night, she had done the same thing. Even though my mom and I had been bickering about the party, when I came home that night all I wanted was a hug from her. She had stroked my head and told me that she knew the three of us would work things out. I wanted to believe her, but so far the only thing the three of us seemed to be doing was avoiding one another.

"Teenagers," Olivia said sarcastically.

For maybe the first time ever, Olivia was right. I was a teenager . . . At least, I would be in one more day. I wasn't a kid anymore. I needed to get a grip. I had a presentation to do, and two friends who I needed to make up with from a very silly fight.

I wiped my eyes and smiled up at my mom. "Thanks," I said. "I'm gonna head off to school now."

"I'll drive you," my dad offered.

School was only a couple of blocks away, but it felt even longer without Lara to walk with. I hated passing her house in the morning and then walking on, alone. Maybe a ride to school was just what I needed to start the day off on a better foot.

"And that's why you should book your trip to Mexico," Greg said. "The country's long history and interesting culture make Mexico a must-see for your next vacation."

The whole class clapped, and everyone in my project group smiled widely. Each of us had read our essays in front of our elaborate Mexico poster. The poster had turned out really well. Everyone had worked together — even Marty.

We sat back down in our seats, pleased with our presentation. I peeked over at Becca and Lara, but neither one of them was looking at me. I sank down in my chair.

Jordyn and Dylan were congratulating Marty. I sat at my desk, fiddling with the cover of my purple notebook. No one said anything to me.

"Hey, Carly," Alex piped up from behind me. "I think Mrs. Bloom really liked our poster and presentation, right?"

"Yeah," I said, noticing that Marty was smiling at Drew. Gag. I couldn't see his face, but I wondered if Drew was smiling back.

"I think our presentation was the most original, don't you?" Alex asked.

"Yeah, I guess," I said, only half paying attention.

"You should definitely play some of that Mexican music at your party," Alex went on. "That would be cool to dance to!"

I had to smile. At least I had one friend who was excited about my party.

"I'm so pleased with everyone's projects," Mrs. Bloom said to the class just then. "I enjoyed that Mexico one very much. You all did a fantastic job."

At that moment, the bell rang and everyone sped out of class — including Lara and Becca. I didn't even get a chance to tell them how much I'd liked the crepes that they had passed around for the class to sample during their presentation about France.

Like they had all week, Lara and Becca disappeared after dismissal. They were nowhere to be found. I stood at my locker for a few extra minutes at the end of the day, hoping to see one or the other of them down the hall. But they were gone.

I knew that as soon as I got home from school, I'd have to turn on my party spirit. My grandparents, Aunt Jane, and Uncle John would be there. They were all staying at a hotel downtown, but we were having dinner together. I'd been looking forward to it, but now I wasn't in the mood. I felt like one of those Mylar balloons after it leaves the store and bobs out into the cold winter air. Deflated, I made my way home.

"Hello, candy girl!" my grandmother exclaimed as she opened the front door to greet me. She was wearing a neon green warm-up suit and bright white sneakers. My mom always makes fun of her bright color choices, but I love them. Ever since she moved to Florida with my grandfather, Grandma's clothes seemed to have gotten brighter. But I always think she looks cheery.

"How's my *teenage* granddaughter?" my grandpa called from behind her. He pushed his round glasses up on his nose.

I gave them both tight squeezes. I didn't get to see my mom's parents as much as I had when I was younger. Now they spent most of the winter in Florida. They came up north in the spring and summer — and for special occasions, like their granddaughter's Sweet 13.

"How are you, darling?" my grandmother cooed, stroking my hair. "You look so grown-up."

"Well, she's a teenager now," my grandfather said, smiling down at me.

"Almost," my grandmother said, looking proud. "One more day!"

Aunt Jane and Uncle John came out of the

kitchen to greet me, so there were even more hugs. Aunt Jane is my dad's younger sister. He says that they used to fight like Olivia and I do. I find that hard to believe.

"We were just unpacking the party favors," Aunt Jane explained. "There are so many plastic containers!"

"And that box from Candy World weighs a *lot*!" Uncle John chimed in. "Feels more like fifty *tons* of jelly beans."

They led the way into the kitchen. It looked like party central in there! A bunch of plastic containers were lined up on the kitchen table. Large boxes spilled out into the dining room. And my mom was standing in the middle of all the chaos with a clipboard.

"Hi, honey," she called. "How'd the presentation go?"

"Good," I said, a little distracted by the mess. "But the big freeze is still happening," I whispered, trying to let her know about Lara and Becca without anyone else asking about it.

"I'm sorry, sweetie," she said. "Maybe you can talk to them later today."

"I hope so," I said.

But I wasn't so sure that they would want to talk to me.

My mom put an arm around my shoulders and squeezed. "You can fix this. I bet no one even remembers why anyone was angry in the first place."

I didn't know about that. I was pretty sure that each one of us could recall that night very well.

"This is NUTS!" I heard Olivia scream from the dining room. "Did you look at all these boxes?"

My mother and aunt laughed.

"Oh, Olivia," my mom called back. "Don't be so dramatic. We can get all those jelly beans in the containers in no time."

Olivia appeared in the kitchen doorway with her hands on her hips. "No, it's really *nuts*. The boxes are filled with nuts!"

"What?!" I yelped, charging into the dining room. She *had* to be kidding. I hoped she was kidding. Then again, if this was her idea of a funny joke, I was going to kill her.

But sure enough, Olivia was right. (For the second time in one day, no less.) Instead of fifty pounds of colorful jelly beans, there were boxes and boxes of salted mixed nuts!

"I guess thirteen really is an unlucky number," Olivia mumbled.

CHAPTER TEN

While my mom was on the phone with Candy World, trying to sort out the jelly bean mix-up, I ran upstairs to my room. I threw my party-planning notebook on the floor and flopped down on my bed. What happened to my Sweet 13? For weeks and weeks, I had been so worried about Marty coming to the party. Now that was the least of my problems. My two best friends weren't talking to me, and there was a total candy fiasco that could ruin the whole party.

I reached out and grabbed Mr. Teddy. Whenever I felt sad, that little brown bear helped me out. I hugged him and buried my head in my pillow.

There was a soft knock at the door. I heard Aunt Jane's voice.

"Carly, may I come in?" she asked.

"If you want," I said, sniffling.

Barney snuck in the room behind her and jumped up on the bed next to me. I rubbed his ears, happy to see a friendly face.

Aunt Jane sat down, too. "Ah, Mr. Teddy!" she said, smiling. She stroked his head. "I remember when your dad bought him for you. The day you were born, he went down to the hospital gift shop. He wanted you to have a teddy bear in your crib when you came home from the hospital. I think the two of you have been inseparable since then!"

I smiled. "Yeah, he's the best." His fur was a little matted down and his right eye was chipped, but he was still the greatest bear in the world. I hugged him tighter.

"I still have my teddy, Panda," Aunt Jane whispered. She winked at me. "When I'm upset, I still like to give him a squeeze."

"Thanks," I said. "It just feels like everything's falling apart. I had all these great birthday plans, and now everything is ruined."

Stroking my head, Aunt Jane smiled. "There's plenty of time to fix this. Your mom got through to the candy place. They're trying to sort out where the fifty pounds of jelly beans went. Can you imagine how surprised the people were who thought that they were getting nuts?"

"But it was a *nice* surprise for them," I said. Jelly beans are way tastier than nuts, after all. I covered my head with my pillow. "Aunt Jane, your wedding was so perfect. I wanted my party to be perfect, too!"

"Oh, my wedding wasn't perfect!" Aunt Jane took the pillow off my face and tossed it on the end of the bed. "Did you know that they forgot to serve the pastries at the end of the night, and there were pink roses in the centerpieces instead of the peach ones that I had picked out?" She smiled, and her eyes were twinkling. "But no one noticed those small details but me. And you know what? The party was a ton of fun, anyway."

"I guess," I said. I knew that she was trying to cheer me up, but hearing about things that went wrong at another party wasn't really helping.

"John and I got you a little something for your birthday," Aunt Jane said. "I'd like to give it to you now, if that's okay." She got up and slipped out of my room for a second. When she came back, she was holding a purple box with a velvet purple ribbon. "Happy thirteenth birthday, Carly," she said.

The present looked too beautiful to even open. "Thank you," I said.

I carefully tore open the wrapping and lifted a sparkly purple evening bag out of the box. It was gorgeous — and very sophisticated. I loved it!

"Wow," I said, admiring the bag. "This is amazing. And my favorite color! Thank you so much."

Aunt Jane grinned. "I thought you might like it." She reached out and hugged me tightly. "Oh, and look inside," she added.

I opened the bag. Inside was a slender silver tube of lipstick. I pulled off the top. The lipstick was a pale rose color.

"Try it on," Aunt Jane instructed. "I'm pretty sure that's going to be an excellent color for you."

I got up and stood in front of my mirror. Slowly, I spread the lipstick over my lips. The color was just enough to give a hint of pink. I loved that it wasn't super glossy, but gave some shine to my lips.

Aunt Jane clasped her hands together. "I knew it would be right for you! Oh, Carly, you look beautiful."

"Jane," my grandmother said as her head of white hair appeared around the edge of the door.

"Your cell phone has been buzzing nonstop." She handed the phone to my aunt.

Aunt Jane quickly checked her e-mails on the screen. "I'm away from the office for one day," she huffed. Then she turned to me. "It's gonna be okay," she said. "Your mom is taking care of the jelly bean caper, and maybe it's time you called Lara and Becca?" She smiled at me. "Your mom told me about your fight. You know, no one really ever remembers how a fight starts — it's the making up that counts." She gave me a kiss on my forehead and dashed out the door behind my grandmother, cell phone in hand.

After they'd gone, I looked around my room, thinking. My party-planning notebook was lying on the floor nearby, open to the page that Lara had doodled on during lunch a few weeks earlier. I reached down and grabbed the notebook, smiling at the drawing of the dress that Lara had thought I should wear to the party. There was a smear of mac and cheese on the page. I sighed. That day in the cafeteria seemed so long ago. We were all still friends then.

Suddenly, I realized that we didn't have to stop being friends. This didn't have to be like fourth grade, when Martha and Lara and I stopped being friends. Aunt Jane was right. I didn't really care what we had been fighting about — I just wanted to make up.

I rolled over on my bed and grabbed my cell phone from my bag. I held my breath as the phone rang. When Lara finally answered, I almost couldn't speak. I wasn't sure what to say.

How should I begin? *I'm sorry I was such a beast? My brain was taken over by party-planning aliens?*

"Oh, Lara," I cried after a second. "I'm so sorry!"

I held my breath, wondering what she would say. Maybe she'd just hang up on me.

"Me too!" Lara said to my relief. "I really don't like fighting. And I miss you. Plus, your party is less than twenty-four hours away!"

"Oh, don't remind me," I moaned. I told her what had happened with the jelly beans. She said that she would be over right away.

Becca had the same reaction. "Don't move," she said. "I'll be right there."

Within twenty minutes, my two best friends were sitting next to me on my bed.

"I'm really sorry that I got so crazy," I told them. "I guess between the party planning and not knowing if the boys would be coming, I got all stressed-out. I didn't mean to snap at you, and I definitely didn't like spending the last few days not talking to you."

Lara and Becca both nodded and looked down at their hands.

"I wasn't so nice either," Becca admitted. "I'm sorry."

"Me too," Lara said. "I hate fighting!" A smile spread across her face. "But I'm so glad that we're all together now."

I looked down the table. "I didn't want to have the party without you both there," I whispered. I felt tears gathering in my eyes.

Lara gave me a hug, and in an instant I could feel Becca's grip around me, too.

"I meant what I said about this party being for all of us," I told my friends. "I wasn't sure what I was going to do if you didn't come."

We went down to the kitchen. Now that we were reunited, I was hoping we could help my mom solve the jelly bean mystery.

"We have solved the Case of the Jelly Bean Caper!" my mom announced as we walked in. "The jelly beans were sent across the country to a country club in San Francisco. The store will be sending a new shipment to us tomorrow."

"Oh, thank you!" I said, breathing a huge sigh of relief.

"But we'll need everyone's help," my mom continued. "We'll all have to work quickly to fill the favor containers tomorrow afternoon," she said. She looked over at Becca and Lara. "Can we count on you girls to help? We're going to need all the hands we can get!"

"Definitely," Becca said, smiling.

"We can do it!" Lara added.

I felt as if my luck was finally turning around. A little sugar added to sour lemons definitely made lemonade . . . one of my favorite jelly bean flavors!

CHAPTER ELEVEN

I leaned in closer to the bathroom mirror. How was it possible that on the day that I turned thirteen, the day of my party, I would wake up and find an enormous pimple on my chin?

Was this some rite of passage?

More like a cruel joke, I thought.

I raced into my parents' room. My dad was reading the newspaper in bed, and my mom was getting ready to go running. She had on her running pants and sneakers. She runs even in the winter, which I think is totally crazy.

"Hey, birthday girl!" my mom said when I appeared in the doorway.

I didn't say a thing. I just walked over to her

and pointed to my face. I had no words. I was in the middle of a full-fledged panic attack!

"Don't touch it," my mother instructed. "A little bit of cover-up will solve that problem. But don't touch it — you'll make it worse!"

"Listen to your mother," my dad said from behind a section of the paper. "Picking a pimple always makes it worse." Then he peered over the paper and winked at me. "Welcome to thirteen!"

Great.

Mortified, I went downstairs and paced around the kitchen. I wasn't hungry. It was too early to get dressed for the party. And I swore I could feel the pimple growing bigger and bigger.

"Come for a run with me," my mom said as she walked in the kitchen. "It will be fun."

"Fun?" I echoed. I never went running with my mom. She ran marathons and went for superlong runs. Not really my style.

"Come on," my mom pleaded. "It's the perfect time to go. Your grandparents, Aunt Jane, and Uncle John won't be back here until this afternoon. I'd love some time with you before the party. And I think a run might help you get rid of some of that nervous energy."

I looked at the clock on the kitchen wall. At least going for a run would kill some time. "Okay," I said. "But you can't make me go fast!"

My mom laughed. "You can set the pace."

I went back upstairs and dug out my running sneakers. I pulled on some old sweats and stuck my hair up in a high ponytail. I was ready.

The streets were quiet and a little slick from the morning rain, but the cool air felt good. It was a perfect, crisp morning.

"What happens if the jelly beans don't come today?" I asked my mom as we started out down the sidewalk.

"They'll come," she said calmly.

"I don't know," I worried. "I can't give away empty candy containers."

"Running always makes me feel better," my mom said, changing the subject. "Something about the breathing and the pounding of your feet on the pavement . . . How do you feel?"

Surprisingly, I felt pretty good. I was keeping up with my mom, and I was starting to feel calmer. I could kind of understand why my mom likes to start her day by running a couple of miles. But I still couldn't help thinking about the missing jelly beans — and the pimple growing on my chin.

"I think that we should head back for some pancakes, huh?" my mom said as we circled back onto our street.

"Definitely," I said.

For the first time in a long time, I felt as if I was connecting with my mom. Maybe I was more like her than I thought.

My dad and Olivia were in the kitchen when we walked inside.

"I've got some happy birthday–face pancakes for the birthday girl," my dad called.

"Happy birthday, Carly," Olivia sang out.

"Thanks," I said. I had almost forgotten about the smiling-face pancakes for birthday breakfasts. My dad cooks only two things — actually, he flips only two things — hamburgers and pancakes. But he makes both of those very well. And he always makes us smiling-face pancakes with chocolate chips on our birthdays.

"You're not too old for these, are you?" he asked as he handed me a plate.

"No way," I said, sitting down at the table and digging in. I was willing to bet that I'd never be too old for birthday pancakes.

Breakfast was delicious, and to top it all off, Olivia actually let me take the first shower! I guess the birthday spirit can make people do unusual things.

When I came back downstairs after my shower, Barney jumped up on my lap. I noticed that he had a little box tied to his collar! My parents grinned at me as I opened it and pulled out a beautiful necklace. The chain was delicate, and had a small heart with a diamond in the middle. My first diamond! I immediately put it on, and couldn't stop gushing about how much I loved it.

Olivia handed me an envelope. "I thought you'd like this today," she said.

I tore it open, expecting a goofy card signed, "Love, Olivia." That was what I'd gotten last year. But instead, it was a gift certificate to get my nails done at a spa in town. My little sister had picked out the perfect present! "Thanks, Olivia," I said.

Olivia beamed with pride.

"That was all her idea," my mom added.

I turned to her. "Mom, can I use it today?"

My mom poured more coffee into her mug. "Of course!" she said. "I think we should all go. I'll call now for appointments."

"Not me, thanks," my dad chimed in from the other room. I had to giggle.

After they had showered and changed, my mom, Olivia, and I headed for Zen Spa. I felt relaxed as soon as we walked through the door. The smell of lavender reminded me of the lotion in my mom's bathroom, and the white couches around the room looked extra comfortable. There were small vases of bright purple tulips all over. I loved this place!

"Hello," a woman at the front desk said. "You must be the birthday girl! Please, come this way." My mom, Olivia, and I followed her to the back of the room. "Pick a polish color, and then I'll show you to your seat."

I looked at the cabinet, filled with colorful bottles of nail polish. I had never seen so many — there were two whole shelves of reds!

"Maybe a light pink?" my mom suggested, holding up a bottle.

"Hmm," I said, looking over the selection. I picked up a bottle of pink that looked sheer and a little iridescent. I turned it over to check the name on the bottom. "This one seems right. It's called Celebrations."

Olivia chose a bright pink, and my mom went for a deep red. We sat like princesses on the couch, while three ladies in purple smocks did our nails.

"This was a great idea, Olivia," I said. "Thank you so much!"

"Happy birthday," she said, smiling.

Maybe Olivia wasn't so bad.

When we got home, the Candy World boxes were waiting! I raced over to look inside. There they were — jelly beans! — in every color of the rainbow. Jelly beans had never looked so good to me.

"I've just been waiting for instructions on what to do," my dad said, standing in the doorway of the dining room.

"We'll need some extra hands," my mom replied, looking over at the containers on the table nearby. She turned to me. "Can you give Lara and Becca a call?"

As promised, they showed up just as soon as I called, eager to help.

The sound of all those jelly beans being poured into plastic containers was music to my ears!

"Having jelly beans as a party favor was a great idea," Lara said, filling a container with candy.

"But I don't like the white ones with the yellow spots," Becca said. She made a face as she swallowed.

"That's buttered popcorn," I said, smiling at her sour expression. "Not one of my favorites either."

After the favors were finished and packed back in the boxes, I said good-bye to Lara and Becca. As they went home to change, I went upstairs to get ready. My party-planning checklist was all checked off. Now all I had to do was get dressed and go to the party!

I couldn't believe that the time was finally here. Now that my friends and I had made up, the favors were in place, the boys were officially coming, and I had the perfect outfit, I was ready to celebrate. I blew my hair straight and slipped on my purple outfit. For the first time, I felt like a teenager.

Then I put my new tiara on my head, and felt like a princess...a princess with a pimple on my chin!

Just in time, my mom came into my room with her makeup bag. I will forever call my mom's makeup bag her "bag of magic tricks." With only a few strokes of cover-up, the pimple went from being a red flag on my face to being totally invisible.

"Carly, you look beautiful," my mom said. I couldn't help noticing the tears in her eyes.

"Thanks," I said, giving her a hug. Maybe she wasn't such a Momzilla after all.

As my mom walked out, I stared at myself in the long mirror behind my door. A smile spread across my face. I was thirteen and about to have the best party of the year! Who cared if Marty was going to be there? Today was my day.

The final touch: I slipped on my new pair of heels. I was ready to go . . . except that my feet started to throb as I walked from my closet to the door of my room. *The price of beauty,* I thought, trying to imagine what Lara and Becca would say. Then I reached into my dresser and grabbed a pair of socks, just in case.

When we got to the Riverhouse, the staff was busy setting up the back room. On each table was a basket overflowing with candy, and bunches of balloons flying up above. Sylvia had lined the room with big silver buckets of candy, too. It looked amazing!

"Wow," my dad said as he walked in.

"Sweeeeet," Olivia squealed from behind him.

I just smiled.

I spotted Myles at the DJ booth, wearing all black and looking extra cool. He flashed me a toothy grin.

"Hey, there's the birthday girl!" he called, waving. "I got your list of requests — we're all set for a rocking party."

"Great," I said. I looked over his shoulder at the open silver case of CDs, and squinted at the labels on the plastic covers. I began to feel my throat tighten.

"Um, Myles?" I said. My throat was dry and I could barely speak, so I just pointed. I was no DJ, but I was pretty sure that a case full of Frank Sinatra was not going to get my party started. At all.

Myles leaned closer to the box. "Oops," he said, laughing. "I must have grabbed the wrong box from my car. Don't worry, Carly. These aren't for your party!"

I breathed a huge sigh of relief. "I was about to have about my second panic attack of the day!"

And just as I said that, the lights went out.

The Riverhouse was pitch-black.

"No one move!" Sylvia called out. "We'll get the lights back on in a minute."

Was this unlucky thirteen striking again?

What would a dance party be like with no music — and no lights? Squinting in the darkness, I turned around to look for Sylvia. As I did, my ankle wobbled and I lost my balance in my new high heels. I reached out to brace myself . . . and my hand hit a platter of something on the table nearby. Even in the dark, I could tell that I'd just made a huge mistake.

The entire platter hit the floor with a *splat*! I cried out and jumped away, but not far enough. As my eyes started to adjust to the darkness, I could make out some of the damage. I'd hit a platter of mini meatballs.

There was red sauce everywhere.

My heart started racing. Disaster strikes again!

The sauce was on the table, on the floor . . . and on my new purple skirt. I raced into the bathroom, which was barely lit by two exit signs.

Just breathe, I told myself, trying my hardest not to cry.

My mom and Aunt Jane were close behind me, each carrying a flashlight.

"The sauce is really only on the skirt," I told them, shining the flashlight on myself. "We need seltzer and some paper towels."

Even in the dim lighting, my mom looked surprised.

"Mom," I said. "Party Planning 101 involves preparing for disasters."

"I'm on it," Aunt Jane said, running out of the bathroom.

I slipped off the skirt and handed it to my mom. "And blot; don't rub," I told her, reciting the line from the article about "Stains on Site." She nodded and followed Aunt Jane.

Only seconds after my mom had disappeared, Lara and Becca came running into the bathroom, their shoes clattering on the tile. By the light of the exit sign I could see how beautiful they both looked. Lara had on a gorgeous pink tank dress, and Becca was wearing a short black minidress.

"Are you okay?" Becca asked, rushing to my side. "What happened?"

I bit my lip to keep from crying.

"Everything is under control," I said, channeling calmness.

"Here," Lara said as she reached into her bag. "Put on my tennis skirt." She pulled a yellow skirt from her bag and handed it to me. "It's clean," she added. "I didn't go to tennis on Friday after the whole jelly bean fiasco."

I stared at her in total disbelief. She really did carry a magical bottomless bag. I silently vowed that I would never make fun of her oversize handbag again.

"What a disaster," Becca moaned. "The party hasn't even started, and it's already a mess."

"Becca!" Lara cried. "Don't say that." She put her arm around my shoulders. "No one is going to see the sauce on your skirt."

A wave of panic was quickly washing over my calm state. I imagined everyone being escorted into the Riverhouse with flashlights and sitting around in silence, bored out of their minds. I twirled my hair around my finger and wished for a clean skirt and overhead lights. Was that too much for a birthday girl to ask?

"This has to get better, right?" I asked.

Lara sat next to me and held my hand. "The party hasn't even started. We have time to fix all of this."

"Right," Becca chimed in. "The lights will come back on, and your skirt will be good as new. It's all going to be perfect."

I wanted to believe my friends, but being near tears in the Riverhouse bathroom — wearing a tennis skirt! — was far from perfect.

CHAPTER TWELVE

"Guests are here!" Olivia cried as she pushed open the bathroom door. "Two people just walked in." Before she finished reporting what was happening, she caught her dim reflection in one of the mirrors above the sinks. She smoothed out her new black dress and touched her hair, which was swept back into a clip. "Seriously, Carly, you need to get out there."

But I wasn't ready to go anywhere.

I wiped my eyes with a tissue, forgetting that I was wearing mascara. I glanced in the mirror above the sink. Now I looked like a raccoon.

"The lights in the front are working, but the back room is still dark," Olivia reported. "Sylvia put out these little candles everywhere. Actually, the place looks really cool."

"Who's here?" Becca asked.

Olivia shrugged. "Two girls," she said. "I don't know who they are. Dad's talking to them."

Oh, great, I thought. I had to get out there, and fast.

Lara's hand tightened around mine, and she gave me an encouraging smile. "Come on," she said. "Let's go see who's here."

I stepped closer to the mirror and rubbed the black from under my eyes. Then I opened my sparkly bag from Aunt Jane and took out my new lipstick. If I was leaving the bathroom, I was at least going to look good! I did a final check in the mirror.

The pimple was still covered.

My lipstick was on.

I was all set.

Minus one purple skirt.

"Your skirt is almost dry," my mom said, coming back into the bathroom and holding my skirt under one of the hand blowers. "Why don't you go see who's here and then come right back in? You'll be able to put on the skirt in a few seconds."

I nodded. I wanted to see who'd already

arrived! The suspense was killing me. Plus, I had to save my guests the embarrassment of talking to my dad.

Following Lara and Becca out of the bathroom, I stood close to the cake table in the back corner and peered around it. Mariah and Mindy were talking to my dad when Lara and Becca walked over to them. Whew.

Myles must have done something to fix the fuse, because music suddenly piped through the speakers and the lights flickered back on. Just in time! Plus, the candles added a really nice touch to the room, just like Olivia had said. The place looked sophisticated and cool. I looked over at the food table and saw the trays of chicken fingers, mini hamburgers, meatballs, and pasta. My idea of a fancy party was coming true, complete with a real menu — not just regular birthday party pizza.

This was the party that I had dreamed about . . . and it was really happening!

"Carly," my mom said, tapping me on the shoulder. "The skirt is dry. You can put it back on." She smiled. "And just in time — more people are arriving."

I ducked back into the bathroom and pulled the purple skirt back on. Good as new! I checked myself in the mirror. I was ready to greet my guests.

Turning to leave, I saw my mom in the doorway. "Happy thirteenth birthday," she said, giving me a hug.

I closed my eyes. "Thanks, Mom," I said. "For the party, the outfit — everything."

She kissed my forehead. "Go have fun."

As soon as I walked out of the bathroom, Sylvia appeared by my side. "The electricity is working fine now," she said. "Sorry for the scare!"

"Everything is fantastic," I told her. Now that I was back in my purple skirt, the lights were on, and Myles wasn't playing Frank Sinatra, I was feeling better. Much better.

Until Drew walked in.

My heart beat faster. My palms got all sweaty. This was a moment that I had thought about for so long! Right behind Drew was the rest of the soccer team, and they were all dressed up. As they got closer, I noticed that Drew's hair was still wet.

"Happy birthday, Carly," he said.

"Thanks," I said, willing myself to speak. No awkward silences for me tonight — I was the birthday girl! Maybe it was the purple outfit or maybe it was the fact that it was my party, but I managed to ask a question. "How did the game go?"

"We won," he replied with a grin on his face. His green eyes sparkled.

"Congratulations," I said, smiling back. (I wasn't sure if I should confess how closely I watched their team's status during the playoffs.) My insides flip-flopped, and I looked down at my feet — which were throbbing inside my new shoes. I couldn't wait to take them off to dance. I felt as if I was towering over the boys.

"You look . . . um . . . tall," Drew said. I guess he felt towered over, too. "And — and nice," he added, stammering.

I smiled. He seemed kind of nervous, too, which made me feel better.

Ryan came up next to Drew. "This place is cool," he said, looking around the room. "Very cool."

I think that may have been the first full sentence that Ryan ever said directly to me.

At that moment, Myles's voice boomed through the speakers. "Welcome to Carly's Sweet 13," he said. "Let's get this party started!"

A pulsing drumbeat pounded through the room. Becca and Lara came rushing over to me.

"I love this song," Lara said, grabbing my hand. "Come on, let's dance."

And as only Becca could do, she waved an arm

to gather up Ryan, Drew, Max, and Greg. "Come on, this is a great song!" Just as a sheepdog corrals the herd, Becca successfully moved everyone onto the dance floor. There was a disco ball in the center of the ceiling that cast sparkling lights around the room.

All the girls slipped off their shoes before heading to dance. My heels may have been pretty and fancy, but I felt much better with two feet firmly planted on the ground.

Before long, we were all dancing in a big circle. Even though no one really paired off, I was next to Drew. He hardly moved, even though the rest of us were bouncing around to the music. I got the sense that he was way more comfortable on the soccer field than the dance floor. But I didn't mind. He was here, next to me. Maybe this was the candy rainbow after the storm?

And then one of my greatest fears came true.

From the corner of my eye, I saw my dad twirl my mom onto the dance floor! I wanted to duck under one of the tables scattered around the room. I wanted to hide behind the clusters of balloons. I wanted to disappear!

And just as if we were in our kitchen at home, my dad started to slide and swirl and wiggle his hips. My mom laughed and danced along. I tried desperately to signal her to stop my dad from embarrassing me any more than he had already!

"Are those your parents?" Drew asked, leaning toward me. He was so close that I could smell his shampoo. It made my nose tingle and my head spin. But I came crashing back to reality as he pointed to the crazy couple in the middle of the dance floor.

I just nodded. I was speechless. There was no denying that those were my parents.

"He's got some killer moves," Drew said, smiling.

"Is that your dad?" Ryan asked, dancing up next to me.

I nodded again. What else could I do?

"He's a really good dancer," Max added. He shook his head approvingly. "Cool."

Before I realized what was happening, a crowd of my friends surrounded my parents, clapping and cheering them on.

Could they really think it was *cool* that my parents were such dorks?

Just when I thought it couldn't get any worse, my dad danced over to me and held out his hand. Oh, no. I glanced at my mom, then back at my dad.

He had such a goofy expression on his face that I just gave in. I took his hand.

I let the beat of the music take over, and tried not to think of all the eyes that were glued to me. Instead, I kept my eyes on my dad. His goofy faces made me laugh as he danced, and I began to see that his moves weren't actually so bad. He was having a good time — and once I relaxed, I realized that I was, too.

"Great dancing for a great song," Myles said over the speakers as the song came to an end. "Let's hear it for Carly and her dad!"

Everyone applauded as my dad spun me around. I gave him a tight hug.

"Thanks, Dad," I said.

"Promise me another dance later, okay?" he said.

"You bet," I told him. I turned back to dance with my friends, and wound up dancing next to Ryan. Drew was across the floor, and I would have had to make some obvious moves to switch my position. Next time!

"Hey, dancers," Myles said as the song faded away. "Let's get everyone up for some Coke and Pepsi."

"Oh, this game is fun," Lara said. "We played this at my neighbor's bat mitzvah!"

I stood in the middle of the crowd on the dance floor, awaiting instructions. Drew was still across the floor, and I couldn't catch his eye. I wondered what he was thinking. Did he even want to dance with me?

"Grab a partner," Myles instructed. "I need two lines, and everyone should be facing their partner."

Someone grabbed my hand. When I looked up, I was shocked to see that it was Alex! I almost didn't recognize him without his baseball cap on. I didn't realize that his brown hair was wavy and hung down across his forehead. Usually, his hair was matted down from his hat. Without the hat, I could see that his blue eyes had little orange flecks in them.

Alex smiled and pulled me to the edge of the dance floor.

Across the room, I spotted a figure in the red glow of the exit sign. Marty. She was wearing a pink strapless dress, which didn't look silly on her at all.

"I play to win, you know," Alex said, snapping me out of it.

"Me too," I shot back, moving into position for the game.

I was happy that Alex was there to distract

me from thinking too much about Marty. Out of the corner of my eye, I saw Drew drift off to the side of the dance floor. I guessed he didn't want to play.

Myles's voice rang through the speakers. "I'm going to play the music," he said. "And when I yell 'Coke', the left line needs to run over to your partner. Your partner will kneel down so you can sit on his or her lap. When I yell 'Pepsi', the right line needs to run and sit on their partner's lap. If I yell '7 Up', then you dance in your line until I say 'freeze!' Anyone who doesn't freeze is out. Are you ready?"

"Yes!" the crowd on the dance floor shouted.

"Come on, Carly!" Alex cheered from across the floor. "We can win this!"

Becca and Lara were on either side of me. Across from Becca was Greg, and across from Lara was Max. I scanned the room for Drew. Where did he go?

As soon as the music started, I forgot all about Drew. It was hard to think of anything else but Coke and Pepsi! Alex had some good dance moves, and he was the best partner I could have asked for for Coke and Pepsi. By the time the song was over, I was exhausted from running back and forth. We held on for a while, but Becca and Greg eventually won the round. Myles gave them each huge bright blue sunglasses as a prize.

"Do you want a drink?" Alex asked me.

"Thanks," I said, surprised that he thought to ask. "That would be great."

As I watched Alex walk away, I had a weird feeling in my stomach. Before I could even think about what had just happened, Becca and Lara were all over me.

"You looked like you were having fun with Alex," Becca said.

"Becca, she likes Drew," Lara whispered, winking at me.

Becca raised her eyebrows and shook her head. "Hmmm."

Before either one of them had a chance to say anything else, Alex appeared back by my side, handing me a glass of soda. "Not sure if it's Coke or Pepsi," he said with a wink, "but definitely not 7 Up." He laughed. "We'll win the next time, Merrin," he said.

No one had ever called me by my last name. For some reason, I blushed as he walked away.

"Cute," Becca said, beaming at me.

"Who would have guessed?" Lara added.

But I wasn't listening. My attention was on something — or someone — across the room.

Marty was still in the corner, but now she was talking to Drew.

"Have they been talking this whole time?" I asked.

Becca shrugged. "I don't think Drew talks all that much."

"But Marty sure does." Lara giggled.

Myles came over the microphone at that minute, calling everyone back to the dance floor for the limbo. As we all took turns arching our backs and limboing under the stick, I tried to forget about Drew and Marty. But when the song ended, I turned and saw Drew walking toward me.

"Hey," he said. "Do you want to dance?"

I thought I might melt — even though I could feel Marty's icy glare from across the room.

"Sure," I said.

And for once, I really didn't care what Marty was doing.

Drew and I walked onto the dance floor. When we got there, Myles started a slower song. I felt my hands get all sweaty, and I wasn't sure what to do. Drew shrugged and put his arms around my waist, like some of the other boys were doing. I put my arms on his shoulders, and we swayed to the music. I closed my eyes and took a deep breath. It was the moment I had been dreaming about!

But slowly, I realized that dancing with Drew was like dancing with a scarecrow. He was stiff, with no rhythm. To make things worse, he didn't say a thing. He didn't even look at me! He was too busy keeping tabs on his friends off the dance floor to pay any attention to me at all.

This was my magic moment?

When the music stopped, I sighed. I'd learned that lesson the hard way: If I was going to have a magic moment, I was going to have to find a different partner.

"I'm gonna get a drink," Drew said awkwardly. He didn't ask me if I wanted one. Not like Alex had.

When he wandered away, Lara and Becca appeared at my side.

"Not so magical, huh?" Lara asked.

"Not really," I confessed, wrinkling my nose.

"Aha!" Becca squealed. "I totally knew it. Alex, right?"

"Your sixth sense?" I asked, smiling. How could she tell, if *I* only just figured out that I liked Alex? He'd been my friend forever. I never imagined that my magic moment on the dance floor might be with him. Who knew what would happen?

"Well," Becca said thoughtfully, "sometimes these things are not so clear. But I could tell."

"Yeah, right," I said, jabbing her with my elbow. "That was totally unexpected!"

A phrase from one of the party-planning articles I'd cut out popped into my head: "Always plan for the unexpected." I hadn't understood that at the time, but I sure did now!

CHAPTER THIRTEEN

"It's the halfway mark!" Lara said, waving me over to our table. She pointed to her bright pink watch. "The party is going so fast!" She opened the candy container at her place setting and poured a handful of colorful jelly beans into her hand.

"It's already half over?" I asked. From across the room, I watched Alex drink a soda. I couldn't help noticing that he looked cute in his blue button-down shirt and khaki pants.

"This is a great party," Mariah said, breaking into my thoughts.

"And I love the jelly beans," Mindy added. "Awesome theme."

"Thanks," I said, glancing around the room.

Everyone was dancing and eating, and they seemed to be having a good time.

Lara popped another jelly bean in her mouth. "You see, I told you we could fix everything!"

"And there's still plenty of time left to dance," Becca said, shimmying and twirling around. Then she looked over at the DJ platform. "Myles is an amazing DJ. And he's cute, too!"

"Becca!" Lara squealed. She gave her a gentle tap on her head. "Another crush?"

A smile spread across Becca's face. "Come on, let's get back to the dance floor."

"I'm right behind you," I said. I had spent too many hours dreaming about this party not to enjoy every moment. As soon as I got to the dance floor, Myles's voice came over the speakers again.

"We're gonna play another game," he said. "Everyone grab a partner!"

I froze for a moment. There was really only one person I wanted as my partner.

And then there he was.

"Carly, do you want to team up again?" Alex asked, appearing next to me.

"Only if you're ready to win," I said, raising an eyebrow.

Alex laughed, and my stomach flip-flopped.

When I looked around, I saw that Drew was standing with Marty — and he didn't seem happy about it. Weirdly, I realized that I didn't even care.

"Okay, dancers," Myles sang out. "We're gonna play some music, and when it stops, you freeze. But you have to stay with your partner, and if either one of you moves when the music stops, you're both out."

"You're probably really good at this game, huh?" Alex asked.

"Not bad," I said, grinning.

"You don't get three strikes in this game," he said. "So pay attention!"

The music started, and Alex totally surprised me. He swayed to the music and made goofy faces just like my dad. He was just being Alex. The first time we had to freeze, it was so hard to keep a straight face — he kept making me laugh!

Myles put on the bubble machine, and Alex and I tried to pop the bubbles as we danced. When the music stopped and we had to freeze, I felt just like the girl in the catalog photo. This was definitely a magic moment. It may not have been what I expected, but I wouldn't have traded it for anything.

The music started up again, and I tried to mimic some of Alex's crazy moves. When it stopped, we were both standing on one foot with our hands up in the air. One look at Alex and we both burst out laughing.

We were out, but I didn't care.

"You want some food?" he asked, leading me off the dance floor.

"Sure," I said. I tried to think of another time when Alex was so polite. Or maybe he had always been that way, and I'd never noticed? I watched as he walked across the room to the food table.

A roar from the dance floor made me look over and see Myles holding up Becca's and Greg's hands. They had won again!

Just then, I saw Marty — and she was walking toward me. She walked as if the space between us was the plank on a pirate's ship. She didn't look very happy to be getting ready to take a plunge into the cold water.

"Happy birthday," Marty said flatly.

Wondering if her parents put her up to it, I looked around to see if anyone was watching. Nope.

"Thanks," I said finally, trying to channel an older, mature teenager. "You having fun?"

"Yeah, it's a cool party," she said. Then she smiled, looking a little bit relieved. I guessed I wasn't that frightening to talk to.

"Beats your Fairytopia party, huh?" she said, cracking a little smile.

I couldn't remember the last time that I saw Marty grin like that. She always had a lip-glossed pout on her face, like Dylan and Jordyn. I had actually forgotten that she had two dimples when she smiled.

"You had the same party theme that year, too," I joked, smiling back at her. For a split second, it seemed like old times.

"Yeah, well, we were different then," she said. Her eyes shifted to her shiny silver ballet flats.

"Yeah," I agreed. "We were."

And for the first time in a long time, I was okay with feeling different. I had two best friends who had my back. Even when we got angry with one another, we found a way to make up. Not every friendship had to end the way Marty ended ours. In fact, some friendships never ended. And, I thought as I watched Alex carefully pile food on two plates, new kinds were forming, too.

"Well, I hope you have fun tonight," I said.

"Yeah, you too," Marty said.

"Glad you could come," I said. And I really meant it. As I walked over to help Alex with the food, I couldn't wipe the smile off my face.

After a few more songs and a lot of mini meatballs, my parents rolled the cake out to the middle of the dance floor.

"It's time for the cake," Aunt Jane said, walking up next to me. "Are you ready?"

I nodded and followed her to the middle of the dance floor while everyone sang "Happy Birthday." I felt like a movie star on the red carpet. Everyone was snapping photos, and the flashes were blinding. There would be a ton of pictures to record that moment, but I knew that I wouldn't forget what I felt like standing there with my birthday cake. I didn't need a photo to remind me. I smiled at Becca and Lara, my mom and dad, even Olivia. Then I saw Alex grinning at me, and my smile grew even wider.

I closed my eyes and wished that I'd always remember this moment. Then I blew out my thirteen candles. (Plus one for good luck!)

"Everyone out on the dance floor!" Myles said as Sylvia wheeled the cake off to the side to be cut. He put on one of my favorite songs. "If you want to wish Carly a happy thirteenth, then get on out there on the floor."

As the song pulsed through the speakers, I looked around at my friends and family. How did I get to be so lucky? Alex was dancing by my side (really dancing, not just standing there), I had faced Marty, Lara and Becca were still my best friends, and I was finally a teenager.

This was no unlucky thirteen — instead, it was pure sweetness in a rainbow of jelly bean flavors.

Hello, Sweet 13!

check out the
first candy apple
summer trilogy!

ENJoy this special sneak peek at

Wish You Were Here, Liza

by RObin wasserman

Location: 35,000 feet above Ohio
Population: 347 passengers, 23 flight attendants, 2 pilots, 1 yapping Chihuahua in the suitcase under the seat behind me
Miles Driven: 0
Days of Torment: 1

"In the event of an emergency landing, your seat cushion can be used as a flotation device," the flight attendant announced as we took off.

I wanted to raise my hand. *I have an emergency*, I would have said.

I'm on the wrong plane.

On the wrong trip.

In the wrong family.

Stuck in the wrong summer.

Just lend me a parachute, I would have said, *and I'll get out of your way.*

I used to like airplanes. The taking-off part was fun, like a lame amusement park ride. The food was gross, but there was always dessert — cookies or pretzels or candy bars — and, unlike at home, I was allowed to have as much as I wanted. There were people to eavesdrop on, bad movies to watch, and if I was lucky, a pair of gold wings that I could pin to my backpack. It was pretty much the greatest thing ever.

At least, that's what I thought when I was a kid.

Turns out I was kind of a dumb kid.

Don't get me wrong. The plane wasn't the problem. Not the *whole* problem, at least. Yes, it smelled like BO. Yes, lunch was two pieces of stale bread with watery mustard smushed between them. (There was no way I was going to eat any of the other stuff they gave us.) Yes, the Chihuahua in the carrying case shoved under the seat behind me *Would. Not. Stop. Barking.* But I could have handled all that. *If* we'd been flying somewhere acceptable. Like Hawaii. Or Florida.

Or home.

I closed my eyes, trying to imagine that.

If I were home, I'd be at the local pool, stretching out in the sun, wondering whether Lucas McKidd would notice my new purple bathing suit. Or I'd be figuring out what to wear on the first day of camp. A counselor-in-training had to look the part. I would make my best friends, Sam and Mina, come over and —

That's where the fantasy cut off, like someone unplugged the power cord. Even if I *were* home, Sam and Mina wouldn't be there. Mina was at art camp and Sam was at the beach. They were both away for the whole summer — just like me.

"Liza, we have a surprise for you!" my mom had said, peeking her head into my room the day after my birthday. My father peered over her shoulder.

That should have been my first clue. If it had been a *good* surprise, they would have given it to me *on* my birthday, right? Instead of a new calculator and ten rolls of film for the decrepit, non-digital camera that I'd been begging them to replace.

My second clue? Surprises in my family are almost never a good thing.

Surprise . . . we're going to eat nothing but tofu and kale for dinner this month!

Surprise . . . Great-Aunt Marge is coming to stay with us for two weeks, and you *get to share your bedroom with her!*

Surprise . . .

"We're going on a family vacation — for the *whole* summer!" my mother announced, eyes glowing. My father beamed. I buried my head under my pillow, hoping I was still asleep.

I wasn't.

My mom rolled down the windows, and that unmistakable beachy smell filled the car at once: salt, sand, and even a little coconut oil mixed in. I took a deep breath. I couldn't see the ocean yet — the dunes and tall beach grass blocked my view — but I knew it was out there, just past the sign that said "Welcome to Salt Isle." And I was suddenly filled with this twittery feeling. I couldn't wait to get to the house!

Then I had to gasp for breath. The air smelled nice and all. But it was hot out there!

My mom turned down the soundtrack to *South Pacific*. "Sam, call your dad, sweetie," she said, tossing her cell phone back to me. "Tell him we're almost here!"

"Sure," I sighed. "But call me Samantha, please, Mom."

She grinned and looked back at me in the rear view mirror. "I keep forgetting, hon. I'm sorry."

I quickly dialed my dad's work number. It was just about three o'clock — two hours before he had to be on the air.

"Suzanne?" he answered, saying my mom's name since I was calling from her phone.

"No, Dad," I said. "It's me."

"Well, hey there, sunshine!" he said. "Where are you guys? Everything okay?"

"Yep. We're here. Almost. Mom said to call. We miss you."

"I miss you, too, sunshine. But you made good time! Hey, what's the temp?" he asked. (It doesn't take long for my dad to talk weather.)

I glanced at the gauge on the dash. "Ninety-one," I replied. Then I breathed deeply again. "But it feels like a hundred."

"Ooh, scorcher!" he said. "Well, get used to it. I'm looking at the air pressure, and it doesn't look like the heat's going anywhere for quite a while. And tell your mom to buy extra sunscreen. The UV index is only getting higher. Give her a big kiss for me, too, sunshine. And Joshie, too, of course."

I looked over at my brother who was picking away at his nose. I had to swallow hard to keep the milk shake I'd had with lunch from coming up at the thought of kissing him. "Uh, sure, Dad. Of course." (Right.)

"Good. And, hey — save some fun for when I get there, okay?"

I grinned. "Okay, Dad. Love you."

I hung up and turned my attention back out the window. This beach road was a lot different than the ones in New Jersey that I was used to. Where were all the T-shirt shops and ice- cream stands? Where was the amusement park? And the arcade? All this place had were beach houses, as far as I could see.

"So, uh, where's the boardwalk?" I finally asked my mother.

"Oh, I don't think there is one, honey," she said.

"No boardwalk?" Where would Juliette and I hang out? "So what do kids do here?" I asked her.

"Well . . ." She shrugged. "I guess they go to the beach."

Every day? For eight weeks?

"Oh, look!" my mom went on. "You can also play putt-putt."

"Putt-what?" I echoed.

"Miniature golf. See." She pointed to a miniature lighthouse surrounded by various strips of green. She read the sign: "Lighthouse Putt-Putt. Looks like fun to me!"

I sighed. Thank goodness Juliette was going to be there, or this would be a very long eight weeks!

Finally, we turned off the main road. Before I knew it, we were driving toward a big house with a sign on the front that said ISLE BE BACK.

I totally loved it!

"Is that it?" I asked my mother. "Wow, it's pretty cool! I mean, it doesn't look quite as huge as you described it, but that roof deck looks like fun. And it has a pool! And a tennis court, too?" I almost hated to admit it, but this place was going to be awesome!

"Huh?" my mom said absentmindedly. "Tennis court? Pool? Oh no, hon. That's not it." She laughed. Then she drove right by the house and pointed to another one behind it. "There you go. The Drift Inn. That's us." She pulled up and turned off the car's engine.

"Whoa!" Josh cried. *"Big one!"* And he was right.

Or he would have been, if he'd been talking about the ginormous mansion looming in front us and not some three-pointer he'd just scored on his DS game. "Yes!" he added, pumping one fist in the air. "In your face!"

But back to the "beach house." I mean, I'd seen some big houses — Olivia Miner's came to mind — but this thing was out of control. Way bigger than the other house I'd been looking at. So big that there wasn't even *room* for a tennis court or pool around it. I'd assumed it was some kind of old hotel or school or something.

And by "old," I mean . . . a *total* mess.

There were a million people rushing down the street — so many it made me woozy. I struggled to keep up with Auntie Jill, who was practically leaping down Fulton Street. I was way behind her, huffing like I was in the middle of a five-mile run. Lugging the new art supplies box my mom gave me as a going-away present, I felt like I was carrying a plump ten-year-old.

I followed Auntie Jill down the stairs into the cavernous underground station. It was hot down there and it kinda smelled. I made a mental note: *Don't touch anything in the subway.*

Auntie Jill took one look at my face, shook her head, and cracked up. "You'll get used to the subway quicker than you think," she laughed. She handed me a small yellow card, then headed for a turnstile leading onto the platform. "Keep your MetroCard in a safe place, okay? You're going to need it to get to all of the different places you and your class will be traveling for your art assignments."

I watched Auntie Jill swipe her card and push through the turnstile, and then I did the same, just as the train rushed into the station. We walked double time to the yellow line, squeezing past a couple of people. Standing to my right was a girl about my age, effortlessly hoisting an art supplies box twice the size of mine to look at the oversize hot-pink watch on her left wrist. She caught me staring and smiled. I quickly turned my head toward the opening subway door and moved a little closer to my aunt, who was about to make her move onto the train.

There weren't any seats on the train, and because my hands were full with my art supplies and I wasn't used to riding a subway, I forgot to brace myself for takeoff. And what do you know?

As soon as the train pulled out of the station, I went flying into the girl with the hot-pink watch.

"Omigod, I'm so sorry," I told the girl, grappling for the silver pole and trying to catch my footing. I dropped my MetroCard at the feet of a man with sneakers the size of a small canoe. As I fumbled around on the floor trying to retrieve the card, I could feel practically every eye in the car trained on me.

"Um, yeah. The poles are a perfect way to keep that from happening again," the girl said as she grabbed my elbow to help me up. She giggled, so I guessed she hadn't meant it to be mean. I still cringed.

"Here, let me take your art box, honey," Auntie Jill said. "You okay?"

"Uh, yeah, I'm okay," I said, running my fingers over my neon-green miniskirt, swiping at imaginary dirt and trying really hard not to look like a total dork in front of all of New York City.

"Nice art box," the girl said as she moved her hand on the pole to make room for mine. "I saw one just like it at Pearl when my mom took me to buy mine. You an artist?"

I hesitated. I didn't really know what to say back, or even if she expected me to speak to her. And what in the world was "Pearl"? I sure wasn't about to ask her, though, because the girl said it like I was supposed to already know. I settled on a weak "Kinda."

"Actually, my niece is quite talented and well on her way to becoming an artist," Auntie Jill chimed in. She clearly couldn't help herself from bragging about me. Embarrassed, I fought back a groan. "I see you have an art box, too—are you an artist?" she asked the girl.

"I want to be." The girl smiled warmly. "I'm actually on my way to the SoHo Children's Art Program. Today's my first day."

"Really? What a coincidence! I'm an instructor there, and my niece Mina is going to be in the camp, too," Auntie Jill said excitedly. "What's your name?"

"Gabriella," she said, rolling the "r" in her name and giving a little wave. I took a closer look at the girl; she had an olive complexion and long brown hair pulled into a curly mass at the top of her head.

"Well, it's nice to meet you, Gabriella," Auntie Jill said. "See, Mina?" she added, turning toward me. "You're not even at the camp yet and you've made a new friend."

I gripped the pole a little tighter and tossed a halfhearted grin in the girl's direction, then focused my attention on my purple Converses. I'd designed my sneakers on the Converse website all by myself. The funky green stripe up the heel and the starry lavender and neon-pink laces I found at Target made them look super-special. I was wearing them when I got an A on my math final, and when I applied for the summer art camp, which had only fifteen openings, but from what Auntie Jill said, hundreds of applications, so it was safe for me to assume that my sneakers were lucky. My best friends, Sam and Liza, got ahold of them just before we all left for summer vacation and signed their names on the sides with special sparkly white marker, reminding me the entire time they were scribbling not to forget them while I was at my "fancy art camp."

But as for Gabriella? I wasn't sure if she'd be real friend material. Suddenly, I missed Liza and Sam more than ever.

CANDY APPLE BOOKS
READ THEM ALL!

Drama Queen

I've Got a Secret

Confessions of a Bitter Secret Santa

Super Sweet 13

The Boy Next Door

The Sister Switch

Snowfall Surprise

Rumor Has It

The Sweetheart Deal

The Accidental Cheerleader

The Babysitting Wars

Star-Crossed

WWW.SCHOLASTIC.COM/CANDYAPPLE

Accidentally
Fabulous

Accidentally
Famous

Accidentally
Fooled

Accidentally
Friends

How to Be a Girly Girl in
Just Ten Days

Miss Popularity

Miss Popularity
Goes Camping

Making Waves

Juicy Gossip

Life, Starring Me!

Callie for President

Totally Crushed

Wish You Were Here,
Liza

See You Soon,
Samantha

Miss You, Mina

Winner Takes All

POISON APPLE

THRILLING. BONE-CHILLING.
THESE BOOKS HAVE BITE!

The Dead End

This Totally Bites!

Miss Fortune